Alice R. Bishop began reading from an early age and became hooked. From then on, she wanted to create her own stories to make other people happy. Juggling motherhood to a young child and writing was a challenge, but one she overcame with help from supportive friends and family, both online and in person, giving her confidence to continue as she suffers with BPD. Some days, writing was especially difficult to push through with the low confidence in herself.

"Told you I would keep my promise, Luke."

Thank you to Abbie, Sam and Becs, for putting up with my stress.

I would like all readers to donate to the wonderful Team Ben Hammond, as this is a wonderful charity that supports treatment of cardiac arrest in the young, thank you.

Alice R. Bishop

TRIPLE THREAT

AUSTIN MACAULEY PUBLISHERS™

LONDON * CAMBRIDGE * NEW YORK * SHARJAH

A CIP catalogue record for this title is available from the British Library.

ISBN 9781398468764 (Paperback)
ISBN 9781398468788 (ePub e-book)

www.austinmacauley.com

First Published 2022
Austin Macauley Publishers Ltd®
1 Canada Square
Canary Wharf
London
E14 5AA

To my friends and family. Thank you for believing in me when I didn't.

Chapter One

Not all love stories happen in the most conventional way, this story is one such case.

I am late, as usual, my stupid alarm didn't go off, and of course, on my first day at my new job, it wouldn't. I rush around like I have a rocket up my arse. I have a quick shower, towel dry my auburn hair, scrape it into a ponytail and pull on black trousers with a white blouse, my boobs actually behaving in the buttons.

Stupid oversized things!

I put my glasses on quickly. My torturous heels were sure to be killing my feet later so I chuck some flats in my bag and run out of the door, locking it behind me. I run to my trusty little red Ford Fiesta which is older than me, throw my bag onto the passenger seat and speed off breaking every speed limit as I do so. I get to the outskirts of the neighbouring town five minutes from the office according to the satnav, as a cherry on the cake of my shit morning, I have to slam onto my breaks to stop for a red light.

Fuck it!

I finally get to the huge, glass-fronted, masculine-looking building of Matthews Building Corporations and rush into reception, probably looking very red-faced and dishevelled, I speak to the receptionist who is sitting at a large glass desk, typing on a computer. She is a beauty, with blonde hair, very slim and model-like.

"Excuse me, I'm here to see Mr Matthews. I'm his new assistant, where can I find him, please?" I say, trying to cover up my heavy breathing.

"Of course, you must be Miss Delaney, in the lift to your right and floor fifteen. He is expecting you, hope you have a good first day," she says, smiling warmly.

"Thanks." I hurry to the lift and try to take a few calming breaths, my body shaking with nerves, I close my eyes and open them to see that the doors have opened on floor fifteen and a tall, well-dressed man staring at me like I have gone mad.

My heart thuds wildly as I introduce myself to this gorgeous Adonis-like man, he has piercing blue eyes like lagoons in the Caribbean, they almost look like they can see into your soul, his black hair is short and well-kept but is slightly wavy. He has full lips that look like they are waiting to be kissed. He clears his throat and the sound shakes me out of my daydream. I smile widely and kick myself for being so distracted.

"You said your name was Delaney? You must be the new assistant that the board hired."

"Y-yes, sir, sorry, I slept later than I'd planned. I apologise."

Why do I feel so nervous?

"Well, that's okay but don't make it a habit, and Miss Delaney?"

"Y-yes, sir?"

"Please rearrange your blouse buttons, you will be a distraction to the other people in the office otherwise."

He looks a little bemused, but there is a flash of something else that flits over his eyes, it's too quick to pinpoint the emotion. I look down and to my horror, a few of my buttons have come undone, exposing my breasts that are struggling to stay in my bra, I hastily do them up, my cheeks burning with embarrassment.

Stupid oversized boobs and fucking buttons with a mind of their own!

"I cannot apologise enough, you must think I'm a right klutz."

"No harm done." He smiles warmly and I see a hint of a blush on his cheeks, he shakes my hand, sadly I am all too aware of my cold small hands compared to his large warm ones. He shows me to my desk, which matches the receptionists' downstairs. He gives me a walk-through of my day-to-day tasks, such as arranging his meetings and helping him prepare for them, I also have to contact new material suppliers for the building sites to get the best prices, this all seems simple enough for me to handle, so I smile and say politely, "Got it, sir."

He nods and goes back into his office. I stare after him through the glass wall of his office for a couple of seconds before shaking myself out of it and cursing my body for finding him attractive, I do not have time or energy for a man. I start to organise my desk, making it a little more homely by adding my favourite potted lavender plant with its soothing scent. The pot is a beautiful royal blue which reminds me of a certain man's eyes, a picture of me and my closest friends, Luke and Katy, and finally my water bottle. Then, I begin to work by turning on the computer and opening Ryan's diary for the day, writing it down on a bit of paper and emailing him a copy. There is nothing too exciting, just a meeting with the board of investors and a staff meeting, I incidentally end up going to both to accompany Ryan and take notes for him. The rest of the day is fairly uneventful in the wardrobe department and my boobs stay where they should, thankfully.

When I get back to my home, my little black cat, Luna, greets me with a meow and a purr, I stroke her chin softly, fill her food bowl with her favourite food and flop down on the sofa stretching my sore back, kicking the silly shoes off my aching feet, and sigh contentedly. My dinner consists of homemade macaroni and cheese, my favourite comfort food, and a glass of strong bubbly local cider to wash it down. I put the plate into the sink to soak off the sticky cheese residue and pour myself another glass of the tangy liquid, which warms my inside and helps de-stress me. I lay on the sofa and turn the TV on and start to watch the latest episode of Peaky Blinders, my binge-worthy show of the moment, I love the drama of a gangster programme. After a few episodes, I head for a shower, wet my long hair and slowly shampoo and conditioner it. I lather my body in my favourite body wash which is scented with lily of the valley, I rinse off and get out of the shower and dry off. I look in the mirror and see my red star tattoo on my left arse cheek and chuckle to myself.

Why at eighteen did I find the winter solider so attractive? Who am I kidding? Even now at twenty-five, he is still sexy to me.

I go back into the lounge when I am clean and sit on the sofa in some clean pyjamas and continue my binge.

Ring-Ring

I must have dozed off, being that comfy on the sofa for an hour or two, I answer my ringing phone, still bleary-eyed, not reading the caller I.D before I do so.

"Annie!"

"Hello, Tubs, how are you?"

"Oh, shut up you rude bitch bag, I know you started your job today, how was it?"

"It was okay, the boss was nice and took me through it all step by step, what he wants from me seems simple enough."

"I bet that is not all he wants, you seriously need to get laid, the last one was six months or so ago, was he sexy?" He teases playfully.

"Luke, I'm not interested in getting laid, it's too much hard work. But I suppose yes he might've been attractive, but I don't want to put myself out there again."

"That means yes with you, I can read you like a book."

"He was an attractive and successful businessman, yes, but anyone with eyes would think he was."

"I still say you need to get laid, you are turning into a moaning old lady."

"Not interested, it never works out well, the last one turned out to be abusive."

He grumbles down the phone at me, Luke and I have been friends since we were toddlers, he always knows how to push the right buttons to wind me up, we are more like brother and sister sometimes, used to drive our mothers up the wall when we got bickering.

"Maybe that's why you're always uptight, you need a long, thick hard cock to loosen you up."

"Luke, I do not need the hassle of a man right now and anyway, what can a man do, that my trusty rabbit can't?"

He chuckles and tuts at me, scolding me over the phone. "A man is warmer for one."

I giggle and say, "But a rabbit doesn't complain it's tired or cannot be bothered."

"Gross TMI, seriously you need a man to whisk you off your feet and make you happy."

"That's gonna be a tall order with my size, I am not exactly a model."

"Oh shush! There are probably lots of guys who would dribble over your curves and your huge fucking tits, I swear your tits grew over one summer, it was like someone gave you growth hormones."

I grumble and say, "I doubt it, and you are so fucking rude, how are you anyway?

"Don't avoid the conversation, I know you want the whole fairy-tale happily ever after."

"I'm not avoiding it, I'm just tired, hun, I am going to go to bed. I'll speak soon to you as I'm exhausted right now, we have to meet up soon."

He sighs a big breath, knowing not to push the tender subject of my lack of dating as my previous relationships have been worse than toxic.

"Okay, hun, love ya! I will keep you to your promise of meeting up soon."

"Love ya too, can't wait to go out on a piss up."

I pad upstairs, my back sore from sitting at a desk all day, flicking the lights off as I go. I strip off chucking the clothes into the laundry basket and run myself a hot, steaming lavender bubble bath, soaking my sore feet and back. I towel dry myself, humming 'I like it heavy' by Hale-storm to myself, one of the many sexual songs I enjoy, I find an outfit for the next day, a red wrap dress which hugs my curves and cinches my waist in, tights and black flats because sod heels two days in a row, my feet couldn't handle it. I put on my stretched over washed t-shirt and snuggle into bed, I set four alarms to make sure one fucking goes off and wakes me the hell up for work on time, then snuggle down under my duvet and try to sleep. Two hours later, I'm still wide-awake.

Stupid Luke woke me up, prick.

I get up and grab a drink and go for a cigarette outside.

Bad habit, I know but helps the nerves.

As I puff on the cigarette and sit out in my garden, I look up at the stars and recount the constellations I know are Orion's Belt and the Big Dipper, I throw the cigarette butt away then I go back up and fall asleep within seconds, my dreams consist of a familiar man with dark hair and blue eyes.

The following morning, I get to work early to set up ready for the day, to make up for the tardiness of the day before, Mr Matthews walks in five minutes later with a scowl on his face which mars his beautiful features.

"Good morning, Mr Matthews, would you like a coffee?"

"Hello Annette, no thank you, wait! Why are you early?"

"To make up for yesterday's mistake, sir, is there anything you need?"

"Not for now, thank you, and do not worry about yesterday, it happens to the best of us."

The rest of the day is fairly uneventful at work. Ryan's mood improves after he has several meetings with building suppliers. Later, I am invited to a bar five minutes' walk away by one of the other assistants to celebrate my first week and I jump at the chance to get to know my colleagues better. I run into the bathroom to spruce my hair up by going through with it with my fingers to kind of tame my insane hair and apply some red lipstick to match my dress and follow Tina, the girl who invited me to the bar, she chats the whole way there about all the sexy male workers at the company and did I have my eye on any one, which instantly makes me blush. She chats like a parrot about the construction company which is a subcategory to the main company I work for, and how the builders who visit Ryan, whoever that is, in his office are smoking hot and dribble worthy, well in her words anyway, I'll have to wait and see for myself. Tina seems to talk about everything but Mr Matthews, she is very twitchy and wants to know everything about me, it's very odd but I want my co-workers to like me so I put up with it. This woman seems very twitchy, and odd, but I cannot complain too much she has taken the effort to invite me out.

I walk into the bar and it's dimly lit old pub, which reminds me of weekends out with my darling alcoholic mother and I smile softly because I love this type of place as I enjoy the kinda people that drink here it makes me feel safe, I am so distracted by my surroundings, I nearly walk into a hulking bear of a man.

"Oh shit, I'm sorry!" I squeak softly.

His hands hold me still so I don't fall with my clumsiness.

"It's okay sweetheart, I wasn't looking where I was going."

I nearly choke on my tongue as I look at him properly, he must be six-foot-five-plus, from his form-fitting shirt his body looks like he is built like a tank, he has chestnut hair tied in an unruly bun on the back of his head and stubble on his chin, his eyes are as blue as Mr Matthews if not a bit darker. He smiles a cheeky grin and lets me go, making sure I am steady on my feet, before walking off to the bar.

Tina leads me to the bar chuckling at my obvious embarrassment, checking her watch repeatedly and says, "So newbie, what's ya drink?"

"Cider preferably please or any spirit, I'm not fussy but I'll warn you I'm a cheap date."

She orders our drinks smiling widely at the bartender and I find us a seat at a nearby table, my eyes keep wandering to the man I bumped into, Tina comes over with our drinks and notices my staring then keeps giggling in my ear about ogling someone already, I laugh and blush deep red.

"I am not ogling, simply admiring a good-looking man."

"Oh don't get so defensive, I do not blame you with that one, but he is a little rough around the edges, I think he has had a bit of a rough start."

"How so?"

She ignores my question and continues to glug her drink like a fish, within seconds her fruity cocktail is demolished. About ten minutes pass and I am already on the second margarita of the night which Tina insisted I tried, Mr sodding Matthews walks in, I swear my ovaries want to explode when he walks up to Mr muscles and embraces him, then starts chatting like old friends, my body cannot take the amount of sex appeal in the room. Mr Matthews notices me staring and waves me over, Tina nudges me to go, I shakily stand and by some miracle, I don't end up on my face, which is always a bonus with me and my accidental tendencies.

"Annette, this is my friend, Max."

"Hello, Mr Matthews, and Mr…Erm Max, nice to meet you."

They both chuckle heartily and Mr Mathews smiles at me.

"You can call me Ryan outside work."

"Yes, Mr…Er Ryan."

"Did you enjoy your first couple of days at the company? You seem to have settled in well."

"Yes, I did, I am really enjoying learning the job, I love being busy."

He smiles a wide genuine smile and my eyes flick to Max and he looks pleased as well, he notices me looking and grins, I blush scarlet and look down, I make my excuses and goodbyes, both men take turns in giving me a warm embrace, they smell amazing which makes me have to bite back a moan, I then slowly walk back to Tina who bombards me with questions about what they said and did, like she is a sodding detective.

I spend the night drinking and dancing, the drunker I become, the more my hips sway and my inhibitions disappear. I excuse myself to Tina, who is checking her watch every five minutes, making me more and more uncomfortable, I stumble my way to the bathroom, I look up through my eyelashes as I pass the two men, the hungry look in their eyes could almost make me melt into the floor. When I reach the bathroom, I splash cold water onto my face to cool my red cheeks and then wipe away my smeared makeup with a tissue to look more presentable, I rush to get back to the dance floor but Tina has left when I reappear, I go to the bar and order another drink, a bit miffed that she left, but it was odd how often she was looking at the time, maybe she had a date to go to.

After nursing my second pity drink, I feel a presence behind me and spin round to Ryan and Max behind me, they are both chuckling to themselves as they help me to stand and they gesture to the bar door, my whole body wobbles as I walk towards it, the men take one of my arms each and carry me to keep me stable.

Ryan mutters softly, "There's a taxi outside to get you home and it'll bring you to work tomorrow, you are absolutely pissed as a fart."

I grumble under my breath about controlling men and white knights. The cold air hits my face and the alcohol I have consumed swamps me all at once and then everything goes black.

"Fuck, she's out." I hear Max's harsh expression as I lose consciousness.

Chapter Two

Ouch, my head!

I grumble and curse myself for drinking so heavily the previous night. I get dressed begrudgingly in some black trousers, a white blouse and some ballet flats, I trudge for the door and head to work. I open my front door to find a black sedan looking car parked in my usual place. A tall, suited, older, well-dressed, looking man exits the car.

"Miss Delaney, my name is Charles. I am here to take you to work, Mr Matthews insisted as your car is still at the office."

I smile courteously and get into the stupidly luxurious car. Sitting at my desk with an extra-large caramel coffee in my hands, that I made Charles stop for, I'm not ashamed to say I got it by begging as Charles was told to bring me straight into the office. As I try to function as well as I can, Mr Matthews walks in looking chipper as ever. I frown, looks like he doesn't suffer the dreaded morning after like I do. Grinning like the Cheshire cat, he says loudly, making my head pound more, "Rough night, Annette, enjoying the caffeine, are we? Here, this'll make you feel better."

He hands me a warm parcel, confused, I open it to find a fresh bacon and egg sandwich, I take a bite and moan loudly, almost obscenely.

"If I knew it would get that reaction, I'd buy you one every day."

Blushing profusely and choking on my mouthful, I smile up at him, muttering apologies and thank yous, he saunters into his office chuckling loudly. After eating my breakfast, I start to feel better and more like a human.

A few hours pass, I start to pack up my things and get ready to go to lunch when Ryan Matthews in all his suited glory, looking like a fucking God, sticks his head out his office door and calls me inside. Puzzled, I go into the office and he says looking like a lost puppy, "Annette, I apologise for this, but would you work with me through lunch? I'll get the lunch and you help me with this speech I have tonight? It's for a charity gala."

"Y-yes, of course, it's not like I have a hot date."

He looks shocked, I fire back with, "I'm joking, sir, I haven't had a date in six months and that was a disaster."

I slap my hand over my mouth and turn beetroot red in utter embarrassment.

"I don't know why I said that, sorry Mr Matthews, please forget I said that, stupid motor-mouth I am."

"Well, if it's any consolation, mankind's missing out, you are quite the catch."

I try to hide my embarrassment and giggle.

"Tell them that, I seem to be an arsehole magnet."

His face turns serious, he grips my chin and tips my head to look him in the eyes. He whispers, "Don't ever doubt you are a confident, beautiful and strong woman, who any guy would be lucky to date."

Then a mask comes over those striking blue eyes and he starts laying papers out for me to read. We spend all of the lunch and most of the afternoon on his speech, he lets me leave early when his speech is complete as a reward for helping so much and he leaves as I do to get changed for his gala. When I am at home, I have a hot bubble bath to relax in, as well as a charcoal facemask. Sighing to myself, I sink into the hot, sweet-smelling liquid and enjoy the peace and quiet. After my relaxation, I decide to go out for a walk, I put my yoga pants on, my trainers and tie my hair in a ponytail, I've never been a slim girl, probably a size sixteen most of the time, but I'm happy with my body, just seems to be everyone else who doesn't approve.

I walk through the woods that surround my little two-bed house, listening to the birds and the wind rustling in the trees. Plugging my headphones into my phone, I put my music on and continue walking, *Move Your Body* by Darkest Days blaring in my ears, I start singing softly while looking at all the beauty in the valley of the woods, enjoying the wildflowers and the scent of the forest. Breathing deeply, I close my eyes and sit down on the edge of the steep valley, probably looking like an idiot, I nod my head and wiggle my hips to the beat while singing a bit louder than before, really getting into the song.

A hand touches my shoulder and I nearly fall into the valley, my eyes fly open and I see Max grabbing the tops of my arms to stop me from falling, I'm holding onto his arms just as tightly, I wrench my headphones out, my body shaking as adrenaline simmers through my body.

"Are you trying to kill me?"

He laughs softly, "No, I saw you on the edge wiggling and the noise coming out of you, I thought you were in pain or maybe a nearby animal was."

"Cheeky sod, that's just fucking rude!"

He laughs even harder, his face lighting up and I shove him, as well as my five-foot-five frame can, anyway.

"Max, how come you are in these woods anyway, don't you live in town?"

"I go jogging in these woods as I find it more peaceful than in town."

I smile at him and look down and notice that my yoga pants are now covered in mud.

"Great! I'm plastered in mud." I giggle then I wipe my hand onto my leggings and then Max's chest and run away laughing like a mad woman.

"Now you are too, payback for the comments about my singing."

He catches up to me easily, chuckling loudly, "And I'm the sod, eh?"

He puts a muddy hand on my cheek softly, making me look like I am in camouflage war paint.

"On my face! That's a low blow."

"You look like a little warrior now."

I pout and glare at him, like the toddler I am. "I am not little!"

"Compared to me you are."

I stalk off grumbling about giant men and their egos, the size of a bloody planet.

Max's laugh follows me out of the woods, he shouts his goodbyes and I head home.

The following morning, I had off work, so I decided to have a self-care day with a trip to the nail salon; I chose a pale pink gel manicure with acrylic tips, afterwards, I went and got some box dye for my hair, as I fancy a change to replicate my new job, I pick up a blood-red dye to match my fiery personality. When I get home, I dye my hair and spend the afternoon curled up on the sofa watching a film playing with my newly dyed hair. That night, I get my works clothes ready for work the next day.

Ding-Ding

My phone alerts me to an incoming message from a number I do not know.

Did you enjoy the mud bath yesterday? Was it like being at a spa?

I frown at my phone as the message is obviously from Max but I don't remember giving him my number. I cautiously reply.

Who is this as I do not recognise this number?

I slip off my jeans and t-shirt, my bra and underwear, then slip into an oversized shirt with some soft shorts to sleep in, falling asleep within a matter of minutes.

Ding-Ding

I pick up my phone to reply, my eyes adjusting slowly to the light and see a picture message from the now known number, it's a picture of Ryan and Max with their faces mashed together looking very, very drunk. Giggling, I snap a picture, reply with my tongue out, trying to hide the fact I am in bed and type a message under.

I guessed it was you, Max, but how'd you get my number? Ha-ha.

I lay my phone down, slipping under the covers of my bed, I snuggle down and go to sleep for the second time. Two hours and fifteen minutes later…

Ring-Ring
What the hell?

Grumbling about who the hell's ringing me, I answer without checking who it is.

"What?"

"Is that any way to talk to your boss's business partner?" Max slurs down the phone.

"Hi, Max, sorry I was asleep, are you okay? You sound funny."

"Shit, sorry, Erm…sorry, you weren't replying to my texts so I was worried, Ryan gave me your number after your drunken episode, when he got you a taxi home, but please don't be mad at him, I asked for it as we had such a laugh

20

yesterday I didn't think you would mind, fuck it! I think I am seriously drunk right now." With comedic timing he hiccups and I hear a thud, followed by a very slurred, "Oh fuck! Curb there, I'm sorry Miss Delaney just fell off the curb."

"It's okay, Max, I was just confused, and it was great seeing you, well until you insulted my height." I giggle like a sodding schoolgirl.

How can I be this bloody embarrassing?

"Sorry about that, well kinda sorry, anyway." He chuckles softly and I swear to God his soft chuckle makes me melt, it's all husky and sexy.

"Max, how much have you two drunk tonight? You sound very worse for wear," I laugh loudly.

"Too much, I bet Ryan's gonna be hanging tomorrow, I will be too, I'm not looking forward to using the power tools and the heat."

"Oh dear…better go to bed now with a pint of water and some pain killers so it's not too bad to go to work with."

"Okay, Ma'am, feeling strict are we?"

I blurt a laugh, "No, Max, I am far from assertive, I just care too much for my own good."

"Hm, not assertive good to know, for future reference." He suddenly sounds serious, which takes me by surprise.

"Max, why is that good to know?"

"No reason." I can almost hear his stupid, cocky, but kinda sexy, grin over the phone.

"Max! Tell me!"

"Nope, now go to bed. You have work in the morning with Mr grumpy head."

With that he hangs up, I grumble loudly but do as I'm told.

The next morning, I wake up refreshed after a good night's sleep, dreaming of sexy men with blue eyes and ready for the day ahead, I grab a coffee and a bacon sandwich for Ryan as I remember he is gonna be hungover this morning, to sweeten his mood a bit. Stepping into his office, I place the items onto his desk with a smile, he grins gratefully and practically inhales the sandwich, I notice dark circles under his eyes and stubble on his chin which is out of place on the usually clean-shaven man.

"Rough night, Mr Matthews? Did we overindulge in alcohol?"

I get a grunt for a reply. Raising my eyebrow, I whisper. "Caveman say ugh."

He smirks and rolls his eyes.

"Yes, Miss Delaney, a rough night, me and Max tried to out-drink each other and I am no caveman or I would have come to your house and thrown you over my shoulder for texting Max like the primal beast you take me for."

His voice is full of seriousness.

"Really, Mr Matthews? Sir, is that what a caveman would do or what you want to do, as it seems to me you want to blur the lines a bit," I whisper, feeling a little brave. He stalks round his desk quickly and grabs my waist and spins me so my arse and the backs of my legs are against the desk, I gasp in shock at the sudden break in composure he usually has.

"Miss Delaney, are you testing my self-restraint? Especially at the moment while I am hungover?"

"N-no, sir," my stupid voice shakes a response.

He puts his hand under my chin and lifts my head to look at him, I gasp and his turquoise eyes bear into mine and he says, his voice almost a growl, "Good, as I don't know how much I have left, you make it hard with those delectable curves of yours."

"I apologise, sir."

"Good, now that we have an understanding, please do not push me."

"Yes, sir," I mumble softly.

"Now, Miss Delaney, please return to your desk and email me my appointments for today."

Talking as if nothing happened. I walk away feeling bare, raw, confused, and maybe just a tad aroused.

That feeling of arousal doesn't disappear as the day goes on, I gaze through Ryan's office window watching him pace around his office on the phone, his black suit trousers hug his arse in a sinful way, which makes me stare, I keep shifting in my seat to try and elevate the pulsing between my thighs, I can feel moisture building as I get wetter and wetter.

Ding-Ding

My computer flashes up with an email, I tear my eyes from Ryan's arse and actually read the notification and it's from Ryan.

'Don't you have something to be doing instead of daydreaming? The glassworks two ways. I can see you staring.'

I cough and splutter then get on with my work. My cheeks flamed with embarrassment. I stand after a while to take some printouts to Ryan, I drop them onto his desk and smile as I leave, I can almost feel his eyes burrowing into my skirt as if he can see through it.

Chapter Three

Standing a bit awkwardly in a club, with Luke attempting to be my wingman, isn't fun. I grab us both a drink, I hand him his Jack Daniels and coke and then sip my bottle of fruity cider, I shout in his ear so he can hear me over the music, "Luke, I'm just nipping outside for a cigarette."

He nods and sticks up his thumb letting me know he heard and I walk outside sucking in cold air and allowing my body to cool after the hot stickiness of the nightclub, I stand in a darkened area of the club's garden away from everyone, I take out my tobacco and roll myself a cigarette, just as I put it in my mouth to light, a flame suddenly lights my cigarette and I jump squeaking softly which is replied with a deep familiar chuckle which makes my pussy clench.

"Max! I swear to God, you're trying to kill me." I scold him.

"Hey, I saw you needed a light, was only trying to help."

His eyes trace my body up and down in the darkness how he can see anything I don't know, but I am kind of glad for the darkness as my make-up must be smudged from all the dancing, Luke insisted I do to make guys aroused, apparently.

"Annette, you look stunning tonight, your dress hugs your curves so well it is almost as if the devil himself designed it to lure men."

"How can you see in this light?" I chuckle.

"I saw you on the dance floor with your boyfriend, you looked very happy."

I laugh loudly as he ignored my question and the tone of jealousy makes my heart flutter wildly.

"Luke's not my boyfriend, he's my best friend, no sexuality between us at all, there is no need to be jealous."

"Oh, sorry, but good to know and yes, I am jealous of him."

I take a quick drag on my cigarette, blowing the smoke out gently and he sparks one up, the flame illuminating his handsome features.

"That's good how?" I whisper.

"Because I want to take you out."

"Take me out as in killing me or on a date?"

"A date, of course, don't you trust me, Annette?" He chuckles loudly.

"I do, Max, but even you must have heard how that sounded?" I smile and put my cigarette in the ashtray.

"I better get back to Luke or he will come looking, he is very overprotective like a big brother."

Max pushes me against the wall by my waist and kisses me passionately and fiercely, I moan into his mouth, melting at his touch, but the kiss finishes as quickly as it started.

"I couldn't let you leave without kissing you, you look so good."

His smile makes me want to have him fuck me up against the wall, I blush at that thought and walk back inside to Luke, touching my swollen lips remembering that kiss and trying to wipe away any smeared lipstick before I get a bollocking from Luke for being sneaky.

I wake the next morning to a text from Ryan and Max, as well as a pounding in my skull from my excessive alcohol use the night before. I put my glasses on and read Max's text first.

Hey, kitten, how's the head? Can't stop thinking about the taste of your lips, I hope I get to taste the other set, soon enough.

I grin and reply.

My head is sore today, Mr Muscles, and the other comment depends on how the date goes, and if you are a perfect gentleman.

I then read Ryan's message next.

Hello, Miss Annette, Max has told me that you are going on a date with him, I would like the opportunity to take you out for a date also, you are an attractive lady and I cannot stop thinking about you. Max and I have been known to share women and the thought of us three together is a very arousing image.

I stare at the phone open-mouthed, but strangely turned on, two men who find me attractive, wow, they complement each other, both are tall, but Ryan is clean-cut and well dressed in suits all the time, whereas Max is more muscular and dresses in a checkered shirt and jeans, very different, but both sexy in their own right. I reply to Ryan.

That is an intriguing idea but I don't know how it would work, wouldn't you two get jealous of the other? As you both seem to be the jealous type as Max did not seem happy that I was out with my friend Luke.

His reply is almost instant.

We will never get jealous of each other, I promise, you mean too much to us already and we have learnt to share. Max was jealous of how happy you looked with another man, we want to be the ones to put a smile on your face.

I am gobsmacked at this revelation and am almost drooling at the sexual images that run through my mind, I shakily put my phone down and go for a shower to calm my spiking arousal and to be able to think more clearly.

Bang-bang-bang

I shoot out the shower to the sound of my door being knocked on so loudly. I wonder if the hinges will give out under the strain.

"Coming!" I shout while chucking a dressing gown over my still wet body, I throw open the door to reveal both Max and Ryan who are looking at me hungrily, looking down at my body, I realise that the dressing gown I grabbed in my haste, is only a light cotton one which has gone see-through with the water from my body and it's clinging to my curves, and you can see the outline of my nipples. Squeaking I cover my breasts with my arms and go to slam the door.

"Wait!" They both say in perfect sync, Max puts his arm out to stop the door from shutting.

"Were you trying to break into my house?"

They both smirk and Ryan says, "No Annette, but you weren't replying to either of us and we were worried."

I look at them shocked, I hadn't realised how much they actually cared.

"May we come in, little warrior? We have a lot to talk about."

26

I glare at Max, but point to the lounge, they walk past me chuckling, I race upstairs and get changed into jeans and a t-shirt, when I come down they are whispering to each other, when they see me both of them quieten instantly and smile warmly to me.

"We have come to discuss the terms of this relationship with you," Ryan Matthews says all business-like making me smirk at him.

"What is this fucking *Fifty Shades of Grey*, Mr Matthews?"

Max explodes with laughter, to which Ryan shoots him a glare that shuts him up.

"No, this isn't, Annette." Ryan sighs and actually sounds like a teacher scolding a student, which of course makes me giggle like a naughty schoolgirl.

"So if it's not a BDSM contract, what do you mean, Ryan?" I murmur, confused.

"We both want you, Annette, so we have to schedule time so we have individual time with you, as well as all three of us, and we need to discuss your thoughts on a polyamorous relationship."

The two men look at me expectantly and I look at the floor suddenly overwhelmingly shy and whisper softly.

"I had never considered a poly relationship, I'd heard of them, but never imagined having one myself, as I have never felt attractive for one person, let alone two."

I look up and see both men looking disappointed.

"That was until I met you two, now I can't stop thinking about the both of you, even if I don't understand your interest in someone like me."

Their eyes light up like kids at Christmas and they both rush to me and squeeze me in a huge hug so tight, I have to cough to remind them I need oxygen. Standing on my tiptoes, I kiss Ryan then Max.

"Annette, you are beautiful. Do not ever doubt that."

I smile at them both.

"I will be both of yours then, and will you stay with me tonight and watch crappy TV and eat junk food?"

"By the way Annie, nice tattoo, what is it?"

"It is the winter soldier's star from his metal arm, anyway, how the hell did you see that?"

"Your dressing gown was more see-through than you think, and you like your men a bit dark then, Annie?"

I sigh and roll my eyes.

"Do you wanna come to my room and watch telly, then?"

They both laugh and nod like Churchill off the TV advert. We lay in my bed, which is a bit of a squeeze with two huge men and a curvy woman like myself, but it is the happiest I've been in a long time, we fall asleep holding each other.

Chapter Four

The past two weeks have been amazing, the three of us have gotten very close. We have only spent one night apart in the two weeks. Surprisingly, we haven't had sex, which is excruciating as I swear my ovaries are going to explode with arousal if I don't have an orgasm soon, but I'm afraid battery operated will not be enough, I guess Luke was right.

I walk into the office whistling *Back to You* by Twin Forks. Ryan walks out of his office and gives me my job for today, we are keeping our relationship private at work so that people don't think I only got the job due to it, but we do send flirty messages through text during the day. I start typing a draft for an email to send out in Ryan's place for a charity auction he isn't attending but has donated a substantial amount to. He is taking me out instead with Max for a surprise date, Ryan comes and reads the draft over my shoulder and okay's the email and I send it off, he whispers into my ear. "Only two days till the surprise date, don't forget to pack enough clothes for two days."

I look up, puzzled. "Why enough for two days?"

Ryan's reply is a tap to his nose telling me to wait and see, I huff and mumble under my breath. "I want to know."

"I know, just wait and see, you'll love it."

I spend the next ten minutes trying to guess in my head. Nope, nothing seems like something they would both do.

Ding-Ding

I look at my phone and there is a message from Max.

Only a day and a half to go now.

This fucking countdown is doing my head in, I need to know.

I quickly type a very begging message back.

Please, Maxy, tell me.

I reply, sounding like an utter brat, but I don't care at this point.

Annie, I am not telling you no matter how sexy you sound when you are bratty, it makes me hard as a board.

I blush just as Ryan walks out of his office.

"Miss Delaney, may I see you in my office?"

Dragging my feet, I follow him into his office and shut the door behind me, Ryan presses a button on his desk and the blinds shut on the glass and door of the office.

"Annette, stop trying to wear Max down into telling you, it's a surprise."

I pout like a child and nod. Ryan stalks around his desk and gently grabs my lip with his thumb and forefinger.

"Don't pout, Max and I have a weakness to brattiness in common, carry on and I will bend you over my nice wooden desk and spank you till it hurts to sit at your own."

I want to moan, the thought of that makes me instantly soak through my underwear.

"Annette, don't look at me that way I already want to fuck you till we both can't walk, but I do not want our first time to be in my office, I want to hear every moan, gasp and breath you take, which I can't here."

My knees go weak at the thought of that, and I have to hold the back of the door to keep me upright.

"Yes, sir," I whisper softly. "Is there anything else, sir?"

He shakes his head and he readjusts himself, I smile to myself as I leave the office knowing I make him as hard as he makes me wet.

Ding-Ding

A picture message from Max with his tongue sticking out and a text below.

Haha, I told on you, did you end up with a pink arse? If so, I'd love to see it.

Sadly, not this time, but Ryan's definitely uncomfortable with the raging hard-on he had, maybe I should make you even.

I giggle as I type my reply, then go back to work.

Ding-Ding

If I continue to hear you giggling like a naughty schoolgirl, I will drag you in here to be spanked till you cannot sit at your desk, so don't giggle anymore. I'm hard as it is, you are not helping that fact.

It's from Ryan, I nearly giggle at his text.

Ding-Ding

Try me, little warrior, and both me and Ryan will give you a pink arse, that is a promise.

I hide behind my computer screen and blush so Ryan can't see me through the windows of his office. I breathe slowly and calm my blush and sneak off to the bathroom, I shut myself into a stall and undo a few buttons at the top of my blouse so my breasts are on full display in my push up bra and take a picture and send it to both Max and Ryan with the caption.

How red is my arse gonna be for this?

I then do the buttons up and go back to my desk, feeling very naughty.

Ding-Ding. Ding-Ding

Both reply within nanoseconds of each other with the same word.

VERY!

I quietly chuckle and go back to work, and eat my lunch at my desk so I can finish all my jobs early and won't have as much to do for tomorrow, so I might be able to leave work early and pack. I finish work and go home alone, which kills my ego a little, but Ryan said I need as much rest as I can get tonight and tomorrow so I am ready for the weekend away. I get home then indulge in a long warm soak in the bath and have a glass of Asti. When I finally emerge, I look like a wrinkled prune. I find my fluffiest pyjamas and snuggle into my warm bed and dream of my gorgeous men naked and sweaty.

I wake to a pulsing throb between my thighs, and I release a shuddering breath, I look at the clock to see it's two am, I strip off and lay back into bed and reach into my drawer for my trusty vibrator. I turn it on and let the vibrations touch my bundle of nerves.

Knock-Knock

I bolt upright and chuck a dressing gown on and turn the vibrator off. I throw the toy on the bed and rush to the door and open it.

"What are you doing, Annette?"

"Ryan, what are you doing here at two am?"

"You called me and I heard heavy breathing and moaning, were you masturbating?"

I blush and nod, damn it! I pocket dialled him. He rushes into the house, slams the door and pushes me against the wall, his lips press to mine roughly, almost hungrily, I moan and he pulls my dressing gown off and he looks at my body and his eyes glaze over with lust.

"Wow, Annette, you are gorgeous. Those curves are to die for, but Max and I own your pleasure, not some battery-powered thing."

"Ryan, please." My voice comes out in a breathy plea.

"Please what, Annette?" he says with a huge smirk.

I moan with frustration and bite my lip.

"What do you want, Annette?"

"You."

He caresses my neck softly with his fingers, I shiver softly and squeeze my thighs together.

"Annette, do you want me between those thighs of yours?"

I nod frantically and pull his hand to the lips of my pussy so he can feel the dampness there, he groans and picks me up and takes me to my room. He lays

32

me on my bed and picks up my vibrator, I blush heavily, I take it from him and put it back into the drawer, I turn back to him.

"Annette, is that puny little vibrator enough for you or do you crave more?"

"More please, so much more!"

He pulls my legs apart and gently touches the outer lips of my vagina with his fingertips and I buck my hips in excitement.

"Wow, you're very responsive to my touch, I cannot wait till Max and I are both touching and filling you."

"Mmm, yes, Ryan."

He lowers his head and licks up my moist slit and sucks the bundle of nerves, to which I moan loudly and writhe with pleasure. Lifting his head he softly murmurs, "Now, Annette, listen to me, I am going to make you cum then we are going to sleep as me and Max have decided that we are taking you on the surprise date early tomorrow as we can't wait, so be a good girl and cum."

He slowly pushes his index finger inside my pussy and taps the most pleasurable spot inside of me.

"Fuck! No one's ever found that spot." I gasp.

"Shush, Annette, cum hard."

He sucks hard on my clit and pumps his finger in and out, I can feel my walls tighten, I can feel my body edging to orgasm. Suddenly, Ryan adds a second finger inside me and my body explodes with intense waves of pleasure.

"Ryan!"

I scream loudly and he licks up my juices, I continue to convulse every time his tongue touches my sensitive flesh, his fingers tightly holding my hips in place in a bruising grip.

"Ryan, stop, no more! You're going to make my head explode."

He chuckles and softly blows on my tender skin, which makes me jolt.

"Now, how are you gonna cope with both me and Max? You are so reactive."

"It's been ages since I last had someone else make me cum, I'll have to adapt quickly as I am very excited to try."

"I'm glad to hear that, now come with me."

He leads me to the bathroom and runs the shower, he removes his clothes and pulls me into the steaming shower. I sneak a peek at the sizeable package this gorgeous man is supporting. He lathers his hands up and washes me than himself, he then dries us both and takes me back to bed.

"Sleep now, Annette, you won't get much tomorrow."

I snuggle into him and kiss his slightly stubbled cheek, I giggle. "Goodnight, Ryan."

He leans over and takes the vibrator from the drawer and puts it into his suit pocket, which is slung over the chair next to his side of the bed.

"You won't be needing this again, goodnight, Annette."

He falls asleep with his fingers over my star tattoo, as if he is trying to cover my obsession with Sebastian Stan.

Chapter Five

So I'm in a car blindfolded, with Max and Ryan in the front and me in the back seat.

Great, no serial killer vibes here.

"Can I please take this sodding thing off now? It's itchy."

I get laughter as a response, we are en-route to this mystery date weekend and I'm bouncing in my seat to get there and see this amazing place they won't bloody tell me anything about. I can hear that the car is now driving on gravel, I try to reach and take the blindfold off and a pair of hands stop me.

"Try that again and you'll be handcuffed, too."

"But, Max…" I whine.

"Wait," They both reply in sync, as usual, bloody stupid stubborn bastards.

The car rolls to a stop and I hear the men exit the car and the door next to me opens, and a pair of hands gently help me out of the car and slowly walk me across, what I'm guessing is a gravel drive and up some wooden sounding steps.

"Guys, please let me look now."

"In a second, madam impatience."

I feel a kiss where my neck meets my shoulders and I shiver in anticipation of what's to come, a pair of hands wind around my waist and hug me tightly, another reaches for the blindfold.

For a split second, I'm blinded as the blindfold is taken off, I blink as my eyes adjust.

Holy shit.

I'm standing in a huge log cabin, actually, a log cabin is an understatement, mansion-sized wooden house is more accurate, with what looks like marble flooring in the kitchen and thick, plush carpet everywhere else. I look around in awe at this beautiful place. There are stunning furnishing throughout.

"Wow, guys, this is amazing, I can't believe somewhere like this is in the UK."

"Do you like it, little warrior?"

"Like it? I never want to leave."

They both grin at my statement.

"Would you like a tour?"

I nod and Ryan takes my hand while Max goes back outside to collect our bags. Ryan gives me a tour of this huge place. There are five bedrooms, all with en-suite bathrooms, plus a family sized bathroom, a massive kitchen that looks like it belongs in a showroom somewhere, a huge comforting lounge, and a games room. Apparently, there is lots of ground on the property, but Ryan says that's Max's domain and he will show me later. The thing that stands out is the master bedroom, the size of the bed, jeez, it's like three super kings joined together, the sheets look so soft, and the en-suite has a huge bath that could fit ten people in.

I think I'm going to enjoy this trip.

I'm gobsmacked at the size of this place, I stroke the smooth cool marble worktop in the kitchen as Ryan and Max discuss what to do next.

"Little warrior, can you ride?" Max asks, looking me up and down.

"Well, I can walk and turn, but not much else. I had a few lessons as a child, why?"

"Okay, here's the plan, Ryan you can cook lunch slash dinner while I take Annie here to the stables to meet Vincent."

"Fine with me, Max, but don't take forever."

Max leads me to a set of sliding doors at the far end of the kitchen diner and we step through onto a decking. We step off the decking and walk down a worn path through some trees. We walk through a wooded area for a few hundred yards and come out to a clearing with a barn and a paddock in it.

This stables, as Max called it, is luxurious enough to be a glamping site, there are stables on either side of a path through the barn, a stable hand nods to Max.

"Mr Romano, are you and your companion riding today? I'll tack Vincent up for you, and who should I tack for the lady?"

"Thanks, Jim, I think Delilah would be perfect for Miss Delaney here. Annette, this is Jim. He looks after the horses while Ryan and I are in town."

I shake Jim's hand and smile. Jim walks off to tack the horses up.

"I'm glad you're wearing jeans and boots today, my little Viking, perfect for riding."

Jim exits a stable at the end with a huge black Friesian stallion, he is stunning, well-groomed and walks very proudly.

"Max, here's Vincent, I'll just tack Delilah up for you."

I look at the horse Max is holding and gently stroke his mane.

"Wow, Max, he's beautiful. How tall is he?"

"About seventeen and a half hands."

I gently stroke Vincent's soft velvety lip and he snuffles my hand. I hear a bolt from a stable open and I look down the path to see a pure white (grey in technical terms) mustang plodding beside Jim.

"Maxie, did you know I love mustangs?"

"Annette, the way you went on about your favourite film as a child being Spirit, of course, I knew, but Delilah is a sweetheart who is well behaved and perfect for you."

We mount our horses and walk out of the barn at a leisurely pace and walk around the huge paddock.

"Wow! Max with all the trees and countryside here how do you ever leave?"

"I have no idea, but Ryan and I are tempted to keep you here hidden from the outside world for our own."

"I might just let you, it's beautiful here."

Max dismounts and opens a gate for us and we walk through the woods for a good hour before heading back. At the edge of the woods, I dismount to pick some wildflowers and give them to Max to carry as I don't trust myself to ride one-handed.

Ring-Ring

Max answers his phone.

"Yes, Ryan, we are on the way back so don't get your knickers in a bunch."

He shoves his phone into his pocket and grumbles.

"The arse hung up on me."

I giggle and walk through the door of the barn before Max and I dismount. My legs feel a bit wobbly, I haven't ridden in probably five years, Max helps me back to the house.

"Shouldn't we take the horses' tack off?"

"Nah, Jim will do it in a bit."

We walk back to the house slowly as my legs are shaky, as Max opens the door, a waft of food entices me in.

"We are back Ry, you can stop panicking."

"Yeah, yeah, come to the table, please."

We wander into the kitchen and the tables have been laid out beautifully with a white tablecloth and beautiful white peonies in a crystal vase and plates filled with my all-time favourite meal, teriyaki chicken and sticky rice with steamed vegetables. I take my seat and smile at my handsome men and dig in.

"Is that nice, Annette?"

"Yes, so good," I mumble with a mouthful.

Ryan blushes with pride and smiles softly.

Max is practically inhaling his food like a starved beast.

"Max, really you are starved."

Max raises his head and shrugs, I giggle and snort. We continue to eat for a few moments in silence, but it's a comfortable one, I gaze at my men and observe their differences. Max is broader and has more muscle mass than Ryan, whereas Ryan is a slender build but more elegant than Max's ruggedness. I smile to myself and finish my amazing meal. We all chip in on the clearing up, Ryan washes, Max dries and I put away with directions from the guys. We then settle on the enormous sofa, which is seriously comfy and watch a few episodes of Peaky Blinders, with me cuddled up between my men. Both the men start making jabs at the show, about the gang violence not being realistic and how those guns do not have that range etc., it makes me chuckle at how in-depth they are going instead of just enjoying the drama and romance of the show.

Chapter Six

I wake suddenly, not remembering going to bed.

How the hell did I get here?

I sit up and see my men asleep on the floor at the foot of the bed.

"Max! Ryan!"

They groggily lift their heads, rubbing their eyes and yawning.

"Get in here now, I'm not letting you sleep on the floor, and besides, I'm cold."

They walk over like zombies and Max climbs in and starts hugging my front, Ryan hugs my back, I smile, snuggle down and I sigh happily. They smell amazing, Ryan smells like citrus fruits, whereas Max smells like pine trees and a woodsy scent, I am in heaven. When I wake again, I feel cold, I look at either side of me and I'm alone.

"Max! Ryan! Where are you?"

They both come running.

"Annie, are you okay? I'm here, I'm here, what's the matter, little warrior?" Max asks, looking worried.

"I woke alone, I was scared you had left me, I kinda struggle with abandonment issues."

Max hugs me tight and kisses my hair.

"Hey, Annette, we will never leave you ever, we promise."

"Guys, I know we haven't been together long, but I have to say I love you two so much."

"We love you, too," Max says smiling while Ryan nods. I've noticed Ryan's not the most talkative.

Max kisses my lips softly, I feel the bed move behind me and Ryan starts to kiss and nip my neck, his breath tickling the sensitive part of my neck, he bites harder leaving a mark to mark his territory. Moaning softly, I kiss Max back and Ryan reaches around and starts playing with my boobs, squeezing and tweaking my nipples, which causes me to jolt and squeal.

"Do you like that, Annette? It certainly sounds like you do."

I moan softly and nod. The pair slowly strip me of my pyjamas, and then Ryan drops to his knees and kisses up my thighs leaving a trail of love bites as he does so, while Max tweaks my nipples as Ryan did before, but Max's rough, calloused hands from his physical job stimulate my nipples more, causing me to gasp and bite my lip. Max pulls my lip from my teeth.

"I want to bite that lip, warrior."

I gasp and blush. Ryan reaches my pussy and licks the arousal of my folds, I moan and my hips buck. The men lift me to the bed and lay me down, they both strip and I swear I drool.

Max's chest has a large tribal tattoo over his left pec which trails down to the delicious v muscles above his sizeable package which is currently standing to attention. Ryan is more sleek and slender with just as sizeable package bobbing gently. Max is the first to move towards me, he licks my nipples to make them hard and sensitive. Ryan is next to approach my body, he kneels between my legs and pushes his index finger into my wet, tight pussy, causing me to buck my hips once more. Both the men groan at my pleasure, Ryan thrusts in and out of me and I feel my pussy tighten, a ball of pleasure building in my stomach, my breath comes in hard harsh pants as my body gets close to release.

"Cum, Annie," Ryan commands. I explode with white-hot pleasure, my moans blur into a long, unintelligible sound. Max lets go of my breasts and moves into the spot Ryan was in.

"Are you ready for me, little warrior?"

I nod desperately and he tests my wetness with his finger then licks my arousal off his finger, he almost growls in approval.

Max positions his hard member at my slick entrance, he thrusts into me hard causing me to shoot up the bed slightly and to moan. He still's inside me, he's balls deep as the saying goes.

"God, you're so tight and warm."

Ryan positions himself by my head and I open my mouth to receive his large dick, the head of it glistening with pre-cum, I lick the tip and enjoy his subsequent moan. Max starts thrusting hard and fast now while I suck Ryan's cock hard I feel another orgasm building, I writhe with pleasure and suck even harder.

"Cum over my cock and make Ryan cum down your throat."

Their pants make me leap over the edge and shudder with the second powerful orgasm of the night, Ryan's cock stiffens, my hand joins my mouth to increase his pleasure, then it explodes with white strands down my throat, I swallow quickly and a salty taste hits my tongue.

"Oh, warrior take my cum."

Max roars as he ploughs into me and I feel his large veiny cock pulsate, he kisses me deeply before laying next to me and then Ryan disappears to the bathroom and comes back with a warm flannel and gently cleans the apex of my thighs. He throws it onto the floor and gently kisses my cheek and whispers.

"Have a quick nap. It's my turn in your pussy next, and I want to tie you."

I nod, intrigued by Ryan's statement about tying me, and what that entails. I turn my head and look at Max, he's already snoring softly, I giggle and snuggle into his back and Ryan holds me from behind, his hard-on digging into my ass cheeks, he gives my tattoo a quick swat. I smile to myself and snuggle down between my two men.

I wake up before them, hop into the huge bath and relax in the warm bubbles, the scent of my favourite bubble bath lingers in the air. When I ran the bath, I noticed that one or both of my guys had been very thoughtful and acquired all my usual toiletries, even down to my obscure hair mask. I lay there for a while, soothing my aching muscles from the earlier exertions.

"Annette! Annette! Where are you?"

I suddenly hear a frantic sounding Ryan.

I quickly jump out of the bath and run into the bedroom without a towel and covered in bubbles.

"I'm here, why are you panicking so much?"

They both run into the room panting and looking very worried until they see my state of attire, their faces softening to large smirks.

"Well, Miss Delaney, I certainly like this look, and I'm pretty sure Ryan can agree it's the best look we have seen on you yet."

Ryan slowly nods and licks his full lips, he stalks towards me with a look in his eyes that is filled with an insatiable hunger. I step back, unable to make eye contact with his desired look at me.

"Not so fast, I am due my turn in that delectable pussy," Ryan growls, almost animalistic in tone.

I gulp and push my legs together as a spike of arousal hits my body.

"But I'm wet," I complain.

I hear a chuckle from Max.

"You are going to be wetter when we are through."

I look up at Max and he has a salacious grin on his face.

Ryan pushes me against the wall, I gasp at the sudden coolness of it touching my back.

"I went gentle on you, Annie. Ryan's the rougher of the two of us."

Before Max could finish his sentence, Ryan's right-hand clasps around my throat, not enough to impact breathing, but enough for me to feel it. My knees almost buckle at the sensation, the only thing holding me up is Ryan's hand. His lips smash into mine roughly, his tongue demanding my lips to part, a small squeak escapes my lips as I thought Ryan was the straight-laced of the two men.

They do say that you have to watch out for the quiet ones.

"Ryan, I think she's enjoying this."

Max's comment comes across as husky, I look over to him and he's naked stroking his cock with hard deliberate strokes, his eyes hooded as he watches Ryan take what he wants. Ryan pushes my legs apart with one of his knees, with his hand which isn't occupied with my neck, he strokes down my body then grasps my boobs, pinching and squeezing my nipples.

My voice a breathy moan as I exclaim. "Ryan, fuck!"

He swiftly removes his hands and lifts me up with more ease than I have ever been lifted and sits me on the edge of the bed. My eyes flick up at him, his eyes a sea of hunger and desire. With one finger he pushes me backwards so I'm laid with my legs off the bed, he kneels in front of me and pulls my ankles apart.

Click-Click

I sit bolt upright and try to move my legs, to no avail.

"They are just ankle cuffs so you cannot close your legs to me."

Ryan explains delicately, but very deliberately.

I lay back down and try not to squirm.

"Stay still or I will pin your arms, too."

"Ryan, I think you should anyway, leaves her unable to stop us from taking our pleasure."

I whimper softly in anticipation of what's to come.

Something cold touches the inside of my thigh and I squeal, Ryan grabs my thigh in a silent warning, I, still awaiting his next move.

A cold what feels like a metal pole is inserted into my now dripping pussy, then Ryan stands admiring his handiwork.

"What now?" I ask panting hard. He holds his finger to his lips and then kneels beside me and takes my nipple into his mouth and sucks hard, making my hips buck but the restraints make it difficult. The cool metal object then begins to vibrate, causing a gasp and a moan to fall out of my mouth. His hand traces down my body to my wet pulsating clit, with a deft, precise movement he pinches then massages the bundle of nerves causing a loud moan to escape my lips.

"Ryan, if you don't fuck her soon, I will."

Comes a gruff statement from Max.

Ryan nods and quickly removes the item from my pussy, he then moves to the bottom of the bed between my legs and uses his fingers to explore in and out of my pussy.

"Ms, you are so fucking ready."

Ryan declares. With one hard and swift movement he thrusts into me causing my whole body to shift up the bed, he grunts in exertion as he thrusts into me like a wild animal, my head thrashing side to side as I'm dizzy with pleasure.

"Cum." He gasps out, as if my body is well trained. I explode with an intense orgasm screaming his name and Max's.

"Fuck, I'm going to mark your body as ours more, so no other man will come near."

Ryan thrusts speed up causing me to mewl in erotic fashion, he pulls out and his thick white seed spurts out covering my lower abdomen and part of my ribs. He sags to his knees panting hard, Max then lets out a grunt and I see his seed cover his hand.

"I just took a bath."

I chuckle softly. Ryan with quick precision, undoes the cuffs and picks me up bridal style and takes me into the bathroom and drops me unceremoniously into the bath. I cough and splutter when I resurface.

"That's a bit bloody rude, you two could at least join me."

They both jump in and chuckle at my drowned rat looking hair.

Max grabs my soap and begins to wash my back with soft circular motions, I sigh softly and whisper.

"A girl could get used to this."

"Good, because we are yours now," Max whispers into my ear.

We wash each other, then dry ourselves slowly, Ryan puts a pair of boxers on and goes in search of food, while Max and I lay on the bed chatting about the upcoming week ahead.

Chapter Seven

After our very hot, raunchy weekend, we head back to work and our boring normal lives for a few days. On Wednesday, Max comes strolling into the office looking very concerned, he stops at my desk and kisses me on the forehead and gently strokes my fringe out of my face.

"Is Ry in the office?"

I nod and he storms into the office slamming the door closed, I see through the glass Ryan shoot up from behind his desk his hands gesturing wildly, I can hear that they are shouting at one another but cannot hear what's said. Max then points and me making me sink deeper into my chair nervously. Ryan then looks up at me, his eyes filled with worry and concern, his in-office phone then rings and he places it to his ear while Max is pacing like a caged animal. My heartbeat pounds in my ears as I start to panic. Ryan slams the receiver down, then throws the phone across his office. His hands rake through his hair and he continues to talk to Max, a bit calmer than before. Max trudges out of the office looking deflated.

"Annie, Ryan and I are going away for a business meeting for a few days, will you be okay?"

I nod quickly and smile softly.

"Yes, of course, is everything okay?"

He huffs out a breath and nods, he bends and kisses me with such force it feels like a goodbye, he walks away, shoulders hunched and looking defeated.

My computer dings with a notification.

Please book Max and I a flight to Sicily, for an ASAP departure.

I quickly book the flight and email them over, my hands shaking as I do so.

"We won't be gone long."

I jolt in my seat, not hearing Ryan approach.

"Fucking hell, Ryan! Did you have to sneak like that?"

He grabs my arms and lifts me into an embrace tightly. I return his tight embrace and whisper.

"Why does it feel you two are saying goodbye?"

He shakes his head and looks sadly down and me.

"It's not a goodbye, Annette, we just don't want to leave you alone."

"We will be home soon."

He leaves the office looking rather worried. I nod a goodbye and take my seat again and continue to work, pouting at the thought of not seeing them for a few days.

I head home after my long day feeling sorry for myself, I feed Luna and open the first of many bottles of cider. Earlier in the afternoon, I received messages from both my men saying they had boarded their flight and they would see me soon. Weirdly, though, Max had also messaged saying not to go into work or out alone until they got back which I found strange turn shook it off to him being nervous about going away.

Three ciders in my body are buzzed from alcohol and I start to have my own rave with my music playing, shots are taken from my bottle of whiskey at the back of my cupboard and dancing like there is no tomorrow. I slump back onto my sofa my high wearing off as I start to miss my men, I put my head into my hands and sigh to myself.

Fancy a trip down the local?

I message my best friend.

Already on the way.

Luke always knows when I'm feeling down, I wobble to my room and put on some jean shorts and a vest top and tie my hair back into a messy bun.

Knock-Knock

"It's open," I shout through, I hear the door open and close so I quickly grab my bag and essentials for my trip out. When I go through to the lounge, Luke has his back to me. I run and jump on his back, he pushes me off and turns around.

Fuck, fuck, fuck! That's not Luke.

I scramble back falling to my arse and try to crawl away. The stranger laughs and stalks towards me, "I see why they are so taken with you."

The man's gravelly voice has a strong Italian accent, he is as tall as Max but with darker hair and olive skin, his eyes are as black as night.

"You are beautiful like the belladonna flower, delicate and beautiful, but would kill me given the opportunity."

I struggle further away and try to run away, he grabs my hair causing me to scream and drags me close to him, he pushes his nose into my hair and takes a long sniff.

"Mmm, scented beautifully, too. I wonder how much they will pay to have you back, but alas, it is my boss who had me acquire you."

I struggle and squirm, trying to evade him, my scalp screaming at his rough pulling.

"Who are you? My friend is on the way over, he will stop you," I protest.

He laughs loudly and pulls a rag from his pocket, covering my nose and mouth. A chemical scent burns my lungs and my eyelids start to droop. My body goes limp and I feel the man chuck me over his shoulder and carry me out of my house. His hands grope my arse, I am unable to fight him off, I am thrown into a large blacked-out SUV type vehicle, and he binds my hands and feet and slams the door. Then everything goes black as my body loses the fight against the drug.

I awake in a dimly lit cellar type room that smells damp, I can hear dripping from somewhere and I try to sit up, my head pounds in protest of my movement and I close one eye to try and elevate the pain. My eye searches around the room to see an escape route, there is a large dungeon type door, a small bucket, a sink and the mattress I am on and that's it. I shiver and look down and myself, to find a thin nightdress covering my cold body.

I wasn't wearing that. How the hell did that get onto me?

I hear footsteps so I try and lay down and pretend to sleep.

"Belladonna, my boss has requested to see you, I know you are awake. There is a camera in the ceiling."

I bolt upright and try to charge at the man, only to wobble and nearly collapse as my legs are like jelly. He grabs me roughly and drags me out of the cell and

47

down a dank, stagnant smelling corridor to a large red velvet-covered door. The kidnapper raps harshly on the door.

"Enter."

A loud booming Italian voice comes from within. My protests are ignored as I'm dragged through the door, a large man is sitting behind a huge wooden desk, and he smiles brightly at me.

"Annie, how nice of you to visit us in our humble abode."

The use of my nickname makes me sick to the stomach, I study the man carefully, he wears a well-tailored, black suit with what looks like a real Rolex on his wrist, but I don't miss the gun holstered beneath his jacket.

"Now, Annie, your boys owe me something so I have you as a bargaining chip to make them behave, if they don't, however, I may keep you to make my bed warm at night."

I see red and spit at the large man who could easily be twice my height. He wipes away my spittle angrily, then hits me hard enough on the cheek to make me see stars.

"Now, Madam, I was willing to play nicely, now I have damaged you which will not impress your puppets."

My eyes burn with unshed tears.

"They are not my puppets, I love them."

My voice is shaking with rage. He grabs my chin and forces me to look at him.

"*Mi Amore*, I know you love them, that is why it will be so fun to break you. If they don't pay up their debt to me, I will make them watch as my men take turns."

I scream and kick out at him, he raises his eyes and looks at the man that took me.

"You'd like that wouldn't you, Giovanni?"

The sick bastardised prick actually grins and nods like a fucking idiot.

"*Si*, sir, please, sir."

I cower away and cringe.

"I am Alessandre, my dear."

The boss man explains, a bit nicer than before, then he clicks his fingers and his errand boy drags me back to my cell, licking his lips as he does so.

"I can't wait to taste you."

The creep leers, before pushing me inside, he pulls a knife from his pocket and slices down the front of my nightdress till my breasts are nearly fully exposed. I try to cover myself while he maniacally laughs and slams the door.

Fuck, what the hell is going on?

I pace frantically, trying to make sense of everything. Out of the corner of my eye, I notice a sheet of paper that wasn't there before, I gingerly pick it up and read what is written.

Dear beautiful lady, this is a note to say, I expect you to come to dinner with me every evening or I will revoke your privileges.

What fucking privileges?

I scan my cell looking at the rancid walls and bucket that fuck knows what that's for, I continue to read.

Your darling men have two weeks to repay what they owe or I will claim you for losses, for now, you are my pet to do with as I see fit.

My hands shake with unbridled rage, tears fall and hit the paper smudging the words on it. I take a deep breath to calm myself and throw the paper away. My eyes shoot towards the door as I hear heavy footsteps again and the door is unbolted, it swings open to reveal the creep who kidnapped me, his face shows a sickening grin, I can see his erection through his smart trousers, it causes my skin to crawl.

"Padre says it's dinner time."

He comes into my cell and grabs my arm roughly, swings my head back and my head connects with his nose with a satisfying crunch.

"You bitch."

He screams like a little girl clutching his nose, blood pouring between his fingers. He pulls his knife from his pocket and lunges towards me, I jump away, his blade barely missing my stomach and I run past him, using his lapse in concentration, slamming and locking the door behind me. The idiot left the keys in the lock, I run almost blindly down the corridor avoiding that dreaded red door and get to what I hope is the door to the outside.

I go bursting through it not caring what is on the other side, only knowing I need to escape. My legs scream as I run barefoot across a stony path towards the metal gate at the end of it. My lungs burn as I get to a huge forest, I hear shouts in Italian following me through the thick woodland. I trip and stumble over some fallen trees looking for somewhere to hide.

"Call padre and tell him we need the dogs ASAP."

"Fuck that. I'm not telling him we lost his prize."

The voices are closer now, my heart is in my mouth as I sprint through the trees looking for a way out. Finally, I see a road through the trees and run as fast as I can towards it.

"Fuck shit! She's nearly at the road, catch her."

I hear someone shout, I ignore it and try to get to the road, I hear dogs barking now, my bare feet are in agony from all the sharp rocks and sticks I've run over. My right foot hits the tarmac and I nearly buckle in relief. Said relief is short-lived as I feel hands grab my hair and pull me back into the cover of the woods.

"Gotcha, you fucking runaway."

I look up into a pair of dark brown eyes. The anger behind them is scary, there is bruising forming on his nose already.

Fuck, it's Giovanni.

His bruising makes me feel a bit smug.

Chapter Eight

My body protests as I'm thrown back into my cell, Giovanni follows me close behind holding some coarse-looking rope in one of his hands. He laughs and you can almost see the crazy pouring off him, "You should have cooperated, Annie."

I gag at his use of my name and try to swing a punch at him without success. Rough hands grab my wrists as another man who is with the freak, ties rope to one of my wrists and attaches the other end to a hook on the wall that wasn't there before. The sick bastard grabs the other wrist and ties it to the other wall leaving me pulled in two directions and unable to move.

He struts right up to me till we are nose to nose, he cups my breast, squeezing tightly, making me wince.

"Be glad I'm unable to teach you a lesson."

I try and shrink away from his rotten breath. I pull my arms trying to escape and hit the dirty prick, to which he cackles madly, he grabs my throat tightly, cutting off oxygen, causing me to get woozy and lightheaded, he reaches under my torn nightgown and cups my sex.

"This will be mine soon enough."

He and his assistant leave the room, I cringe at the sensation of his hands still on my body. My shoulders ache from being in an unnatural position, I let my head drop sobbing softly. A few hours later, maybe days, I can't tell, the padre visits me rubbing his hands together.

"Exciting news, Mi Amore, your men got my message and are on the way here, but they don't know I have you here ready, only that I'm watching you."

His voice is filled with glee.

I look up at him, defeated.

"Don't look so sad. You get to see the loves of your life in a matter of hours."

Two frail-looking young women enter behind him, heads bowed in respect to him.

"These ladies are here to wash and dress you ready for your presentation."

They set a large bucket down and cut off the nightdress and begin to wash my dirty, grime-covered body with scratchy sponges that make my skin raw.

"Sir, we need to have her untied to dress her." The younger of the two women requests, she looks about twenty maybe in age.

"Of course, let me call the guard in to put her to sleep first so she doesn't try to escape our humble home."

He snickers to himself and shouts, "Taylor, bring the needle."

I try to fight as he walks towards me with a vicious-looking needle, the padre watches with glinting eyes, when he realises I am gonna right this tooth and nail, he stomps over and grabs my chin as his lackey stabs me in the neck. My eyes go fuzzy and I quickly drift off.

When I awake, I am laid on the dirty mattress, I roll my shoulders, glad for the relief. My breasts feel tight so I look down and I'm in a fucking leather corset and matching panties, like meat dressed for sodding market. My wrists are black and blue from my bounds, I touch my lips as they feel wet and look at my fingertips, damn blood-red lipstick.

What is this man trying to achieve dressing me up like this?

What feels like a lifetime later, the guard from earlier skulks into the cell and holds up what looks like a nasty-looking bat which is wrapped in barbed wire.

"Time to go."

I notice this man has a British accent, unlike the rest of the people I have met here.

"Where are you from? You don't sound like the others?" I ask, curiosity getting the better of me.

"My mama married into the organisation so I grew up in her care in London."

I nod and follow him out of the cell, like a lamb to the slaughter. We walk in silence till we get to a set of large wooden double doors like you see in movies. They both open to an enormous board room type thing with a domineering looking X cross in the corner. I'm led over and secured tightly to it. Taylor whispers in my ear.

"Good luck."

He walks away and sits at the table. The doors reopen to show the padre with two guards behind him.

"Comfy there, dear?"

Then cackles to himself, pleased at himself for his joke, before seating himself at the head of the table.

I turn my head as well as I'm able towards the door as I hear loud shouting in Italian, the doors crash open to my gorgeous men stalking through it, they both look dishevelled and unshaven. Max looks straight at me and I see the sadness in his eyes.

"Do not go near my prize or I will remove your hands."

Max's eyes lock into the older man and the look he gives him is one of pure, unadulterated hatred.

"Your prize is ours and ours alone."

His voice is like a razor's edge.

Ryan sits down without a glance at me and my heart sinks.

He doesn't want me anymore.

"Welcome, gentlemen, now you have admired my property, it's time to discuss your debt. I want ten percent of Matthews Building Corporations and all the loans repaid for the excavators I purchased for you."

Max paces up and down muttering in Italian and flapping his hands about in wild gestures, which I have never heard him speak before today.

"Speak up, boy!"

The older man bellows.

"Do I have to get Giovanni? I'm here to teach the bitch a lesson, *he* wants to, after she broke his nose. It is going to cost me thousands in repairs."

Two sets of eyes lock onto me looking rather proud, but their business masks all too quickly reappear.

"That will not be necessary, sir."

Ryan whispers fairly respectfully.

I bow my head and listen to the negotiations, I hear my Ryan say he will pay in full in a few days and sell one of the excavators to sweeten the deal.

After an hour or so, they all stand up and shake hands.

"Thank you, boys, for clearing the debt. You may take your plaything with you.

All parties nod and my men approach me.

"Wait! I have changed my mind, I will organise Miss Delaney's delivery to you."

The men sigh, sounding frustrated, and look at me worried, but nod.

"What the fuck? You two are leaving me here, with this prick?"

"That is no way for a lady to converse, I will make sure you reach your men in one piece, I swear on my life."

My men leave the room and my heart breaks into a million pieces, I sob. Brokenly tears stream down my face, ruining the make-up the women applied earlier. Padre saunters over and grabs my chin.

"Don't fret dear, you'll be with them soon. Let's hope Giovanni doesn't decide to take his fill of your body first."

He walks away, chuckling loudly. Taylor rushes over and undoes my restraints.

"He will make sure you get home, Ma'am. Don't worry, he just wants to make them sweat a bit first because they took so long to pay their debts."

My body collapses to the floor out of exhaustion and Taylor carries me to my cell, murmuring soft comforts to me. He lays me on the mattress and covers me with the scratchy blanket and leaves me to my sadness.

After a while of me pacing my cell, when I finish crying, the lock slides open on the door, I pin myself to the far corner, anxiously waiting to see who it is. It's the slimy cock sucking Giovanni, looking rather pleased with himself.

"Time to go, you little bitch. I hope that you like a bumpy ride."

He smiles grotesquely, grabbing my arm roughly and groping my chest so I cannot move, stabbing me with a needle as he does, I bite him hard enough to leave a large bleeding semicircle on his forearm.

"You fucking whore!" He roars, slapping my face hard enough to make me see stars. For the millionth time the drugs take hold, I collapse out cold.

Chapter Nine

Ouch, my skin is sore!

My skin is red raw when I am awake in a dark, what feels like a wooden crate. The ride is a bumpy one like I was promised by the slimy prick. Suddenly, we come to a screeching stop, the car door next to my head is opened and the oversized coffin is pulled out roughly making my body flailing about inside.

"Carry the witch up the steps and drop it at the door."

I hear Giovanni spit.

I brace myself against the sides of the box, trying to save some of my exposed skin from the rough wood. I'm jumbled about then dropped roughly as I'm guessing they put the box at the door. I try to calm my breathing so I can hear what is going on.

Knock-Knock

"What do you want? You dirty, disgusting twat."

Max's voice sounds deadly.

"Now, Max, is that any way to talk to your dear brother? We are blood after all."

What the fuck?

"Your dearest Annie has an amazing pussy, I can't wait to touch it again, that star on her arse makes it look even better."

"The fuck? You touched her?"

I shake my head in disbelief at the news I have just heard, I hear thuds and grunts, and they must be fighting.

"You are no brother of mine, blood maybe, but not a brother as far as I am concerned. Our father should have drowned you at birth."

Max spits.

I hear wood splintering above my head as a crowbar is wedged into the lid and I cower into a foetal position trying to protect myself. The lid opens creaking loudly and I blink at the sudden bright light, Ryan looks like an avenging angel with the sun behind him when my eyes adjust enough to focus on him, he looks at me, noticing the state of me and looks pained and disgusted.

"What have they done to you? My sweet Annette, I am here now."

He gently lifts me out of the box avoiding my sore skin as best he can. I look for Max. He is kicking my tormentor in the ribs as hard as he can, there is a man with him holding Giovanni still, Giovanni's men are trying to intervene without much luck, Max is cursing at him in Italian. I turn away and hide my head into Ryan's neck, not wanting to see my captor any longer, the memories of his touch on my body making me want to curl up in a ball and die.

"Ryan, please take me away," I whisper brokenly.

"This isn't over, I will break you. I will make your dear men watch as I fuck your broken body." Giovanni swears to me in an icy voice.

"Like hell, you will," Max responds in an equally dark voice.

Thud-Thud-Thud

I flinch and cry softly as I'm taken away from the abuser.

Ryan takes me into his house and sits me on his sofa, he looks at me sadly and holds his finger up saying one second and disappears into the house, I lay back onto the soft velvety material and close my eyes, and they quickly flick open when I hear footsteps.

"It's only me, Annette, I need to clean your wounds," Ryan speaks to me gently like I'm a baby deer.

He puts a small bowl of warm soapy water at my feet and delicately cleans my cuts and scrapes as gently as he can, they are all over my body from the weeks of abuse. Working swiftly and efficiently, he bandages my arms and calves, then he numbs and stitches a large gash on my cheek then puts a dressing over my cheek. When he is satisfied with his work he hands me two tablets and a glass of water, he guides my hand with the water into my mouth.

"Take these, then you can sleep."

"Where's Max? What's he doing?"

I look around, panicked.

"He will be here soon. He's taking out the rubbish."

Ryan's voice is like razors.

I sigh relaxing slightly then lay down on the super-sized sofa. Ryan covers me with a soft fluffy blanket and kisses my hair softly, I swear I hear him whisper, sounding distraught.

"I'm so sorry, please feel better."

"Why the fuck didn't you kill the fucking cunt?"

"Do you want another debt, this time a live one?"

The hushed whispers wake me from my fitful rest, I slowly sit up and gingerly stretch my muscles screaming as I do so, I slowly walk towards my men's voices.

"Max? Ryan? Where are you?"

They both appear at the lounge door looking concerned.

"Annie, why are you up, you should be resting?"

Max runs up to me and hugs me tightly causing me to wince and stiffen.

"Max, be gentle. She's sore from her ordeal."

"Shit, sorry Annie, I've missed you so much."

I laugh softly and kiss his cheek, his familiar scent calming and soothing me.

"Maxy, I missed you both, too. Ryan. Can I ask? Why wouldn't you look at me at that dreadful place?" I ask curiously, not knowing if I'd like the response.

"Annette, if I had looked at you I would have shot everyone in the room, then none of us would have made it out of there, I had to keep a lid on my temper, I looked at you briefly when the padre said you broke the snake's nose. It took everything in my power not to shoot the padre between his beady eyes."

I nod, respecting his decision, I yawn loudly and lean onto Max as my exhaustion hits me in waves, I hold onto his belt to stop me from falling to the floor.

"Bed now, first door on the right at the top of the stairs is your room."

Ryan says matter-of-factly.

"Aren't you two joining me?"

They both look guilty and shake their heads.

"Annie, you've had a rough time of it lately. We believe you need some space to heal and Ryan and I have some work to do, we will see you when you wake."

I nod, tears in my eyes, I run upstairs straight into the room Ryan said was mine and jump onto the bed and let the tears flow, the memories of the past few weeks flooding my mind, the hits, the gropes, everything.

At some point, I must have cried myself to sleep, my eyes are sore and like sandpaper, I rub them roughly to get the gunk out of them. I pad slowly to the door and go downstairs in search of a cold drink. I find the kitchen after getting lost twice, I open the fridge and find some ice-cold pre-made vodka cocktails and pop one open, and it's snatched out of my hand before the liquid touches my tongue.

"Oi, I don't think so, Annie, Ryan said no alcohol on your painkillers, come on, I'll make you a smoothie that will help make your body feel better and I make the best smoothies in the world."

I scowl and him, pouting my lip out.

"You want me to heal? After the shit I've been through, I need booze, I have mental scars, too."

I complain profusely.

Max smiles fondly and tugs at my bottom lip.

"I know, doll, but not yet, as you're on strong old meds, soon you can drink your pain away, I will even make my famous margaritas for you."

He gathers out the smoothie maker, goes to the freezer and grabs some frozen fruit, chucking it in and begins to blend it together.

Grumbling to myself about male patriarchy, I sit onto the kitchen side watching Max work. He pours the beautiful cerise coloured liquid into a tall glass with ice, he giggles to himself as he puts a cocktail umbrella into it and whispers cheekily.

"Now you can pretend it has your desperately needed alcohol in it."

I glare at him and take a sip.

Holy fuck, that's delicious.

I glug it down, enjoying the taste and the much-needed hydration.

"Holy shit, Annie, thirsty are we?"

I nod and gently explain. "I didn't get many fluids there."

Max looks at his feet sheepishly.

"Sorry, Annie, I didn't think."

Smiling up at him, I kiss his cheek and say, "It's okay, it's over now."

"Max, what did Giovanni mean when he called you brother?"

Max sighs dejectedly and looks sad.

"He was correct, I am his biological half-brother, the padre is our shared father, I was lucky, and Ryan's family out of the kindness of their hearts adopted me at eleven, by that point, my father was grooming Giovanni to take his place when the inevitable happens."

Holy fuck, I wasn't expecting that.

"It wasn't till I turned eighteen did I see my father again, and he offered to help Ryan and I start our business. Being naive as I was, I accepted the offer and he has been making us do odd jobs to pay off the debt. It was when he found out about you and was wildly green with jealousy over our happiness, he wants it paid in full."

"Jesus, Max! Are you okay? I didn't realise I put you two in danger like that."

He laughs and pulls me into a warm embrace, being mindful of my injuries this time. "You are the very breath I take, Annie, I can say without a question of a doubt it is the same for Ryan, you are our very reason for living."

I smile widely and place my hand on my chest, feeling my heart flutter at his beautiful words.

"Thank you, Max, I feel the same for the both of you."

He smiles happily then swats my behind.

"Go rest up, Annie, so I can show you how much I mean those words to you."

I jog away laughing gleefully and take Dr Max's orders and have a long hot bubble bath, then slip into my nice warm bed and conk out dreaming of little, curly dark-haired children.

Chapter Ten

After a few days of much-needed rest and recuperation, Max and Ryan decide to take me out for the day to enjoy the beautiful weather. It's surprisingly warm for an April day. I'm bouncing in my seat, excited for the day ahead.

"Where are we going, you two?"

Ryan turns to face me from the passenger seat.

"Max said you love animals and that is the only clue you're getting."

I frown, wracking my brains for an answer.

"Don't frown, Annie, you'll get wrinkles on your beautiful face," Max jokes.

"Won't you love me when I'm old and wrinkly then, Maxy?"

He bursts into raucous laughter.

"Of course, I will Annie, I don't want you ageing prematurely, and I enjoy your big perky arse."

"Are you saying I have a fat arse, Max?"

"No I am not, it is perfect, it's like a bubble butt."

We pull up to the local zoo, which is about an hour away from Ryan's townhouse, as he calls it. I call it a bloody mansion.

"Oh my God! I haven't been here since I was a child, I used to love it here," I exclaim buzzing with excitement.

"We know, we have rented it for the day, so it'll only be us three walking around it."

I smile like a kid at Christmas.

"Thank you! Thank you so much!"

"I think she's excited, Ry."

Ryan nods in response and helps me out of the car.

"Now, Annette, you have to take it steady today or your cuts will open."

I nod frantically, trying to run around Ryan to get the day started. Max picks me up like a child and chuckles.

"Not so fast, Annie, we are trying to keep your healing."

I sigh and huff like a toddler.

"I'd stop huffing if I were you, Ryan is partial to a bratty woman."

I look at them shocked, I smirk and bolt to the gate, testing my luck.

"Annette Marie Delaney, get back here!"

Two sets of thunderous feet storm after me, I double over panting and laughing hysterically. Ryan chucks me over his shoulder and carries me to a nearby hut that I hadn't noticed. He pushes me in and shuts the door behind us all. Grabbing my neck, he pushes me against what feels like glass touching my bare legs.

Bit fucking strange.

He kisses me forcefully and rips my pretty cotton dress to shreds with his spare hand.

Guess being careful is out the window then.

"Ryan! I like this dress!"

"I'll buy you twenty new ones, fuck I have missed your body."

I hear Max chuckling behind him. Ryan tightens his grip on my neck and kisses me again. Max saunters over and pushes my underwear down and caresses my already soaking sex.

"Mm, Ry, I think she's missed us, too."

Ryan removes his hand from my neck and lifts me so my aching pussy is at his head height.

"Wrap your legs around my head," he demands.

I do as I am told for once, his tongue snakes out and licks the entirety of my opening causing me to shudder. My head leans back against the glass, enjoying the sensation.

"Ry, don't be greedy, share her with me," Max utters, mostly joking I think.

Ryan lowers me down so my feet touch the floor, within nanoseconds, Max grabs for me and plunges his fingers inside causing me to convulse.

"Mm, fuck! So fucking ready for us."

They both take turns finger fucking me, turning me into a mewling wreck.

"Please, guys."

They smirk at each other and then Max lifts me and wraps my legs around his waist.

"Ready, my little demanding warrior?"

I nod frantically with pleading eyes.

He thrusts hard and deeply, causing a desperate moan to escape.

"More?" He chuckles, his eyes show pure hunger.

"Yes, and don't you dare stop."

That is all the invitation he needs to pump in and out as hard and fast as he is able. My screams echo around the hut getting louder and louder. Ryan kisses me as his best friend fucks the living daylights out of me.

Fuck, I'm gonna cum already.

Max feels my walls tightening already.

"Fuck, fuck Annie, cum."

I cum hard and fast, my head flops forward, tucked into his neck as I ride the waves of my intense orgasm, Max's grunts and pants and spur my orgasm on and on. One last hard thrust and I feel him stiffen as he empties his seed into me. He lowers me to the floor and smirks as his cum drips out of me onto the floor.

"My turn now, you say I'm greedy."

Ryan mutters, rolling his eyes and tutting playfully.

He spins me so I'm facing an enclosure that houses tigers.

"Let's show those tigers what they are missing."

Ryan snickers at his own joke.

He spreads my legs and pushes the tip inside me.

"Mm, fucking hell."

I rest my forehead against the cool glass. I open my eyes and I see movement across the other side of the enclosure.

"Ryan! Ryan! There's someone on the other side of the fence over that way."

I look closer and see a terrified looking zookeeper who's looking a bit sheepish at seeing us. Ryan pulls out of me with a sigh.

"I'm never going to get laid again."

He takes his jacket off and covers me with it.

"Go to the car."

Max and I sprint to the car giggling like school kids caught doing something they shouldn't.

"Where's Ryan?" I ask when we are back in the car.

"He's paying off that zookeeper to make sure he doesn't tell anyone what he saw, poor guys got blue bollocks now seeing you in the throes of passion."

I laugh harder and get into the car.

"Max, your cums gonna get on the seats."

He smirks.

"It's not my car, it's Mr blue ball's car."

"Ryan's gonna be fuming if I stain the seats."

"Nah, he will get it valeted, poor cleaner."

Ryan comes stalking back to the car with a scowl on his face that makes me and Max roar with laughter, he opens the driver door and slams it shut.

"You won't be laughing like a hyena when we get home, madam bratty."

My laughter stops as quickly as it started, I lean back in my seat anticipating what's to come or who is going to. The drive back seems slower than the drive out this morning. I stare out at the passing trees and hedgerows, daydreaming about what Ryan is planning, by the time we hit the drive I'm squirming in my seat, anxiously awaiting my punishment.

The car rolls to a stop and I leap out and make a break for freedom, laughing as I go.

"You never said she had to make it easy for you."

I hear Max tease Ryan.

I run through the hallway, nearly bumping into a maid.

"Sorry, sorry," I apologise to her as I run away.

I get to my bedroom and lock the door. I sit hiding under my bed, panting hard. Five minutes pass, no Ryan.

Odd, maybe he has given up, a bit boring.

I sneak out from under my bed, he's not in my room. I creep quietly to my bedroom door and slowly open it, still no Ryan.

Seriously weird.

I leave my door open and go to my bathroom and get undressed and begin to shower.

Slam.

The bathroom door bangs shut, I peer around the shower screen and see a pissed off looking Ryan.

"Ms Annette, you have ignored everything I have asked of you today, what do you have to say for yourself?"

I smile broadly. "I do not like being managed."

He glares at me and grabs me out of the shower, mumbling that he's only trying to help.

He throws me over his shoulder, leans down, turns the shower off and carries me out of the bathroom. When we get into my room he doesn't stop and walks straight out.

"RYAN! I'm naked, someone might see."

"I don't care. They will learn that you are mine."

He continues down the corridor to his own room, just before we enter his room I hear a gasp. Looking up I see it is the maid I nearly ran into earlier, her cheeks are scarlet from embarrassment.

"Ryan, the maid just saw me as naked as the day I was born," I scold him.

Laughing, he says, "Jemma is probably more embarrassed than you are."

He kicks the door closed behind us and throws me onto his bed. While flicking the lock on the door, he removes his shirt.

"Now, Miss Delaney, I have a promise of a punishment to fulfil."

He licks his lips and slowly saunters towards me. Ryan's bed is now wet and bubbly from my naked form but I can imagine it is about to get even wetter.

He strips mouth-wateringly slowly.

"Miss, you have some drool on the side of your mouth," He chuckles darkly.

I wipe my mouth quickly and crawl across the bed to him.

"I don't think so, no touching," He chastises.

I pout.

"That's not fair!"

"I'll bite that lip in a moment, but first lay down."

I lay down and he ties me to the bed firmly, wrists tied to headboard's end, ankles the opposite, so I cannot move an inch.

"That's better, but I think you are underdressed."

I look up confused and he pulls out a blindfold, he covers my eyes and says, "Perfect."

"Ryan! Did you find her? Don't be too rough with her, I wanna keep her."

"Max, if you don't fuck off this instant I am going to drown you in the pool then bury your corpse under the patio."

"Ooooh, temper, temper."

I hear Max's footsteps recede.

"Now that he's fucked off I can have my fun."

I laugh softly and quickly stop it when Ryan pinches my nipple hard.

"Ouch."

"Good, now shush, put that loud bratty mouth on pause so I can concentrate."

I open my mouth to say more and a ball gag is put into it. I grumble around it, complaining about him being grumpy when he has blue balls.

The next sensation I feel is a cold metal object touching my nipples, making them almost painfully erect.

Fuck, that's cold.

I hear a groan as he notices them, he licks each twice then attaches two clamps, one for each nipple. Moving down my abdomen, he leaves a trail of kisses and gentle bites till he reaches the apex of my thighs.

"Well, this is a sight for sore eyes, your wet waiting pussy."

I can hear the smile in his voice.

His fingers touch my clit and tap it hard like a button making me jump, but the restraints make it impossible to move.

"No moving, wait you can't."

He taps it again harder, causing a moan around the large gag. A buzzing sound starts and he pushes a large vibrator into my pussy.

"Mmm, I am enjoying warming you up ready for my cock."

He slides the vibrator in and out of my body, exciting all my nerves and making me impossibly wet.

"I can still see remnants of Max's cum coming out of you on the toy, this is fucking sexy."

Thrusting the toy harder and deeper into me, he groans.

"I don't know if I can wait long enough to punish you."

The toy is ripped out of me and replaced with Ryan's pulsating member.

"No, I can't wait, I have to fuck you till you see stars."

He fucks me like a primal beast rutting, growling and groaning with every thrust of his hips. Behind the mask, I see stars as I edge to the explosion.

"Fuck, cum and milk my dick dry."

My eyes roll back as I cum around his dick, this only spurs him on, thrusting harder and harder till I feel his seed hit my walls with force and he collapses on top of me.

"Jesus Christ, I needed that," Ryan pants into my ear.

He climbs off me, his cock sliding out of me as he does.

"You look so fucking hot with my cum leaking out of you."

He removes the blindfold and restraints with more care than he did applying them and lastly removes the gag. He washes us both down with flannel from his en-suite and tucks us into his bed, I snuggle down with my head onto his chest.

"Ryan, that was an amazing punishment," I whisper dozily.

"I should do it more often then, now sleep Annette, get to sleep."

I smile and close my eyes.

Knock-Knock

"You two get downstairs now quick, you need to see this."

Chapter Eleven

Sat on the kitchen side, when we venture downstairs, me now in more appropriate dress to walk around the house, is a large cardboard box.

"Charles said a courier delivered it for Annie."

I sit on the side next to it and begin to open it, a rancid, rotten smell assaults my nose as I lift the lid.

What the hell?

I peer in nervously and there is a bloody rag package at the bottom accompanied by a blood-splattered letter, Max grabs me off the side and pulls me to the other side of the room, Ryan gingerly reaches into the box and looks inside.

"Max, take Annette into the other room, now!"

I try and fight my way back to Ryan and shout, "No, Ryan, what is it? What's in that box? Tell me."

Max holds me tight to him.

"Ry, what is it?"

Ryan turns his hands caked in blood, his shirt looking like a murder scene.

"It's her fucking cat."

Sinking to the floor, I let out a scream that doesn't sound like my own. Max struggles to lift me and carries me from the room, kissing my hair with feather-light pecks.

"Annie, you are okay, you are safe."

"They killed my cat, my Luna, I'm gonna fucking make them wish they were never born."

He sits on the sofa with me curled on his lap like a small child, rocking me back and forth in a comforting rhythm. Ryan walks in and I look up, tears and make-up streaming down my face.

"Annette, it was Giovanni, it was him, I need to read the letter, but it's addressed to you, may I read it?"

"I don't want to read that filth, you do it," I say, hiccupping over a sob.

Ryan opens the letter, his eyes skimming over it like rockets in his head, and his eyes darken with rage as he reads it.

"Max, your brother dearest wrote Annie a lusty letter."

I shudder at the thought of what that letter could possibly contain.

"Ryan, read it aloud," I say whimpering.

Dear Miss Delaney,

I am writing to you to inform you of my raging hard-on that you have left unattended, my body burns for you. I will be there to collect you in the coming future to take what's mine, the cat was just a warning about what I am capable of.

I hope you are a sensible girl and come to me yourself and save all this hassle.

P.S. remind your keepers we are awaiting confirmation of their successful job in Sicily, as it was cut short because of their demand for you.

Your rightful owner.

I gag as he reads. My body shaking with fear as he reaches the end.

"What job? What's he going on about?"

"As I told you before, my loving father asked us to do odd jobs to repay our debt, for his organisation. That's why we rushed off so quick to Italy to get it over and done with, we had to go stamp out a turf war on Padre's hometown."

"What Italy, Sicily? That's home to the fucking mafia!"

I jump off Max's lap and spin on him, he's looking at the floor not looking at me.

"My father is the head of the Sicilian mafia, Annie. He is a very powerful man."

I pace in front of the sofa, wringing my hands together.

"That means Giovanni is his second, he's going to fucking murder me."

Ryan grabs my shoulders and shakes me.

"That prick will never touch a hair on your head so long as Max and I have breath in our bodies."

I push into him and hug him tightly, fresh tears staining his shirt, I remember my beloved cat's blood on him and run away.

I hide in my room for several hours, before a freshly showered and changed Ryan stands in the doorway.

"Annette, may I come in?"

"Yeah, it's your house," I say bitterly.

I glare at him and he looks hurt.

"Sweetheart, this is all of our home."

Shock covers my face as he's never called me anything other than Annette or Miss Delaney.

"You are as welcome here as we are."

"Ryan, I'm scared."

He sits down beside me on my bed.

"I know, love, but we will protect you, come what may."

I lean into him.

"Don't leave me tonight, please, I want you both here beside me."

Ryan grabs my phone from my bedside table and shoots off a quick message, I surmise to Max and lays down beside me. I drift off to an unsettled sleep, waking briefly to Max climbing into bed with us.

Screaming myself awake, I open my eyes to Ryan and Max shaking me.

"Annie?"

"Annette?"

Both men stare at me with worried expressions on each of their faces. The nightmare of a dark, dank and musty cell slips from my mind as I gain full awareness.

"I'm awake, I'm awake, stop rattling my brains now, please."

They stop immediately and both squeeze me tight to them in a sort of protective barrier.

Knock-Knock

"Mr Matthews, Mr Romano, is all well? The staff heard screaming?"

I hear Charles's rough voice through the door.

"Yes, Charles. Miss Delaney had a nightmare, please inform the staff we are well."

"Very well, sir. I hope the young lady feels better."

"What's happened to Luna's body?" I say in a small voice.

"We have buried her beneath the willow by the pond, we thought she would like to be near the fish."

I nod solemnly and sigh.

Both men release me and get off the bed.

"We will get that bastard for you, Ry and I swear it."

We all slowly get dressed and head downstairs to start the day, even if it doesn't feel like we should. I leave the boys to let them work in the in-home office and go exploring my new home. I find a huge library filled from floor to ceiling with every book imaginable. Next, I find an indoor pool with an artistic mosaic of a dolphin being ridden by Aphrodite at the bottom, with a Jacuzzi at the far end. As I continue to explore, I realise I am totally fucking lost.

Fucking hell.

I exit the door to what looks like a home gym and find myself in the huge gardens.

How the fuck did I end up here?

I sit on a nearby stone bench and look at the rose garden in front of me. Delicate scents of the different roses tickle my nose and make me smile. Roses were always my grandmother's favourite.

Ding-Ding

I check my phone, a message from Luke.

I have not heard from you in weeks since I arrived at your house to find it empty with your door wide open, you better not be fucking dead. P.S let me know you are okay.

Bypassing texting him, I ring him.

"Luke, it's me."

"I know who it is. There is something called Caller ID. But, hell girl, are you okay? I've been worried sick, what happened?"

I let out a huge sigh, not knowing where to begin. In the end, I blurt everything out, from the kidnapping to the package, crying a little when I say Luna has gone, to now telling him I'm lost in this huge house.

"Give me one of the dipshites numbers and I'll ring them and tell them where you are, you pleb, getting lost in your fancy house."

He rings off and within ten minutes, my men come rushing from around the corner of the house.

"Annette, we had Luke call us saying you were lost, why didn't you ring us." Ryan scolds me.

"I was on the phone to him and it just slipped out."

I look at the floor shyly. Max takes a seat beside me.

"You idiot, you shouldn't wander, especially at the moment with Giovanni out for blood." Ryan continues to berate me.

My temper snaps and I storm away into the rose garden and out the other side, grumbling to myself about not being a child. I reach some old, weathered steps that go down to a pond.

This is where Luna must be.

I sit on the last step and look out over the water, watching the ripples from the wind skim over it, creating tiny waves. The huge weeping willow caresses the murky water like a dancer waving its long tendril branches as the breeze pushes it.

Ah, peace.

Not for long.

Snap-Snap

I spin my head round to the sound of twigs breaking beside me and let out a piercing scream, a masked man approaches me wearing dark clothes and heavy boots.

"I told you we shouldn't have let her go off."

I hear Max's voice from the top of the stairs. Sadly, as does the masked stranger, speeds up and grabs me just as I get to stand.

71

"Did you miss me, *Mi Amore*? I can't wait till we get home."

The gravelly Italian man's voice makes me gag.

I try to escape and he pulls me backwards towards the fence behind the pond.

"Annie, Annie. For fuck's sake, Annette!"

I let out a sharp scream, which is promptly cut off by Giovanni's gloved hand.

"Shut up, shut up."

He fumbles and nearly lets me go in his perverted panic. In the end, he gives up and shoves a cloth bag over my head covered in a familiar scented chemical, that shifts my fight-or-flight reflex into overdrive and I struggle harder as my limbs begin to feel like lead, Giovanni's hands wander over my breasts and he rips my bra then bites over my breasts leaving large bite marks, I start to struggle more.

Thud

A dull pain radiates suddenly to my temple and I fall to my knees.

"Thank fuck for that, she's out."

I am vaguely aware of my body being dragged for a few moments before my flight response gives up and my eyes close.

Chapter Twelve

Before I regain complete consciousness, I am aware I am tightly bound to a chair.

Where the fucking hell am I now?

I gingerly open my eyes, cursing the thudding pain radiating through my skull.

"My pet, you are awake, I apologise for the sore head. You kept fighting me."

Ring-Ring

He takes out his phone and grins gleefully at the screen.

"Ah, Maximus Romano, a perfect time to call, thank you, I now have my possession in my grasp."

I hear Max's muffled shouts through the phone.

"Now, now, no need to shout, and you can tell father whatever you like, he is at the bottom of the local river becoming fish food, you are welcome to join him, he wouldn't let me chase my prey, so I shot the blithering old man between the eyeballs."

I swear my eyes are bulging out of their sockets now.

Fuck. Mow he's the head of the fucking damned mafia, I'm dead, kill me now.

"Bye, Max, it's time for me and my new plaything to get acquainted."

Dropping the phone, he then stamps on it, silencing any of Max's protests.

Spinning on his heel, he turns to face me. His features make my skin crawl, especially his sickening grin, he looks like the cat who's got the cream.

He ain't getting my cream if I can help it.

I struggle in my binds, hoping to loosen one. The cheeky twat actually tuts at me.

"I don't think so, Madam Houdini, I've learnt from my mistakes with you, you aren't slipping through my fingers again."

I scream, spit curse and grit my teeth at him, only to make him laugh, "Carry on, my dear, tire yourself out, then you will be more receptive to me, and any way, watching you fight is making me fucking hard."

Stilling instantly, I gaze at him in disgust.

"You are a sick, pervert, dirty weasel."

"Yes, my dear, and by this evening you will be choking on this weasel's fist while I split you in two."

I blanch away from him, shuddering at the thought. My mouth goes dry as he removes his button-down shirt.

Fuck. Max, got him good.

His entire abdomen and a good portion of his back is covered in yellow and green bruises and a long angry-looking cut across his chest which looks like it's barely healed.

"Admiring my chest, my dear?"

His grin is salacious and makes my skin crawl.

"Why would I want to do that, that cut looks nasty, would be a shame if it got infected."

He points to his red, raw-looking chest.

"This I received from your big fuzzy teddy bear, Max," he says, looking at me sadly.

How did he cut Giovanni?

"Confused, sweetness? Your Max is always armed, didn't he tell you why he went to Sicily?"

"Yeah, for a job for the padre."

"Were you told what that particular job entailed?"

I shake my head, confused about where this crazy man is going.

74

"A turf war."

"Your ray of sunshine men, Max and Ryan, went to the Italian island to murder the opposing gang leader's eldest son to make the mob fall apart."

"No, they would have told me. We keep no secrets."

"Oh, you sweet, naive princess. You are in our world now, so grow up, it's not all sunshine and flowers, people die, at least I'm honest about being a monster. Why the hell am I discussing this with you?"

He physically shakes himself and you can almost see the crazy take over his eyes as his grin reappears.

"Now, where were we?"

Knock-Knock

"Boss, your brother and his friend are coming down the drive, Taylor has opened the door ready for them, and I thought you'd like to go to the smoking-room for your meeting."

Giovanni pales and looks rather sick.

"You fucking idiot! Stop them, I told you, if they arrive."

The very ill-looking man rushes out of the room, slamming the door, leaving me bound to the chair.

Trying to escape from the bloody chair, I hear gunshots echoing in the rooms around me. One bullet comes through the door and embeds into the floor a mere few inches from my bare feet.

"Hey! I don't give a flying fuck what team you're on, that nearly hit me."

I hear raucous laughter from the other side of the door.

"That's my girl."

I hear Max's voice.

"Max, Max I'm in here!"

The door splinters open from the force of Giovanni being thrown through it, Max jumps through after his brother's body still pummelling punches into the man's chest.

"Max, Max, I'm here!"

Max's attention shifts to me, Giovanni takes the opportunity of Max's loss of concentration and punches him in the temple, causing him to go out like a light.

"Annette! Are you here?" Ryan's shout reaches my room from somewhere in the house.

"I'm here!"

Giovanni spits blood on the floor.

"Well, my pet, that is my cue to leave, but don't you dare think I'm through with you."

He gets to his feet, wobbling as he does so, and then runs and jumps out the window as if it's the most natural thing in the world, I hear a splash, so there must be a pool below.

I flop my head forward, taking the first deep relaxing breath since being here. A blur of Ryan rushes past the door and skids to a stop sharply.

"Annette, you are okay? I'm so—"

Thud

He trips over Max's unconscious body, hitting the floor like a sack of rocks.

"Fuck. Ryan, are you okay?"

Lifting his head to look at me, his face covered in blood splatters, he crawls towards me slipping and sliding on the wooden floor with his bloodied hands.

My hands and feet are swiftly untied. Ryan assists Max to stand, the poor man looks positively green from nausea.

"Maxy, are you okay?"

He shakes his head then promptly groans at the movement.

"Ryan, let's go home before he comes back with help, which is possible, I cannot believe he shot his own father."

The men shrug.

"Annette, it's not surprising, Giovanni is a crazy son of a bitch."

We arrive home and Ryan puts Max to bed, then the both of us sit in his home office.

"Annette, I am so sorry for snapping at you and making you run, while we were in the garden."

"Ryan, to be completely honest with you, I don't care about that, I need you to do something for me, I need you to teach me how to fight, so far I've survived by sheer dumb luck, and I need to be able to defend myself from Max's delight of a brother."

Ryan waits for my rant to end, looking partly amused, but with hard eyes.

"Sweetheart, Max will hate me if I teach you to fight, he kinda likes being your knight in shining armour."

Heat rushes to my cheeks as my rage boils hotter and hotter.

"What is this? The bloody fifteen hundreds?"

Huffing at me, Ryan gestures for me to follow him. He looks mildly irritated. We walk to the gym and he tells me to sit on the bench at the side of the room and he begins to wrap my knuckles with a white cloth.

"You wanna fight? We are going to spar, so I can learn what you have got."

Standing upright, I bounce on the balls of my feet, rolling my neck and stretching my arms.

"Fine."

I charge at Ryan, trying to catch him off guard, he blocks my smaller frame easily, kicking my legs out from under me, making me hit the floor, knocking the wind out of me.

"Ouch, fuck, dick move."

"No, Annette, dick move would be telling you, that if you do well, I'm gonna fuck you till you can't walk for a week."

I blush hard, wanting to live up to his expectations, the sly fucker then removes his shirt and my jaw drops as I see his abs tense.

"Not distracted, Madam, are we?" He chuckles at his own game.

I shake my head, getting myself prepared to fight.

"Not at all."

I swing punch after punch, throw kick after kick, to no avail. I am unable to land a single hit on the light-footed fucker. I slide to the floor breathing heavily.

"Giving up are we?"

I glare up at him and boot the side of his kneecap and cause his legs to buckle.

"Never," I pant as I lay back onto the floor.

Laughing while panting hard, he crawls over to me, he climbs on top of me straddling me.

"One word of advice, if you're in a real fight, fight as dirty as possible. It'll save your skull."

He flexes his hips, pushing his obvious hard onto my crutch through the thin workout shorts I am wearing, causing me to gasp and moan. His chuckling at my response to his touch pisses me off, so I try and buck him off. I am rewarded by him pinning my arms above my head, he leans down and tries to kiss me, I take my advantage and head-butt him making him jump off me in surprise.

77

"Fuck, that hurt, is your head made of bloody granite?"

"It's not you sarcastic fuck, but you told me to fight dirty, I'm my defence."

I jump up and start to jab him with punches in the ribs and stomach, trying to get the upper hand.

"Fine, you little monster, that's how you want to play it, then."

He grabs me by my right fist as I try and land another punch, he pulls my arm so I'm flush against his chest and he cups my arse cheek.

"Oi, I'm sure you're not meant to feel up your opponent."

"Only when I want to fuck them hard for shaking their arse at me for half an hour."

Slap

His hand connects sharply to my behind causing a loud yelp from me.

"Ouch, that hurt."

Using the hand holding my fist, he spins me so I'm facing away from him and whispers into my ear.

"I'm going to fuck you on the floor of this gym, sod whoever walks in."

"Ryan Matthews, I never took you as an exhibitionist."

"I'm not, usually, but you, Miss Delaney, bring out a primal side of me."

Pushing me to the floor, I hear a zip being pulled down as he steps out of his trousers.

"On your knees, that delectable ass in the air, your tattoo that represents another man drives me wild, I want to cover it in my seed."

I do as I'm told, enjoying this side of my usually stoic lover. My shorts are pulled down along with my underwear, a breeze hits my arse and I shiver.

"Mm, your arse looks amazing in this position, I can see everything I want access to."

With a groan, he touches my wetness with impossible gentleness, causing me to wiggle my hips to get more friction to my body.

"Stay still, this is not going to be gentle, I cannot hold back any longer."

Fuck, he was going easy before.

A primal sounding growl roars out of his mouth as he fills me with a hard thrust sheathing the entire of his large cock in one go, it causes me to scream his name.

"Shush, we don't want to be interrupted just yet, I think Jemma's already had enough of a show of your body already."

I place my hand over my mouth to cover the next moan as he slams into me again.

"Can you take more?"

"Please! Ryan, I can take it."

Pulling out of me he sits back on his knees, I mewl at the sudden loss of his touch, he pulls me backwards onto his waiting cock. He fucks me harder in and out, this position is even deeper than the last. Within seconds, I cum so hard I see stars, this sets off his powerful orgasm causing his forceful seed to coat my insides and my inner thighs, he pulls his powerful cock out of my body and wipes some of the dripping cum over my tattoo as he promised.

"Fuck I needed that, you are so sexy when you are raging and fighting me."

"Well, that's not the idea of me learning to fight."

"Maybe you'll just distract them enough to hand their ass to them."

I grumble and pull my clothes up, very aware of the wetness of his cum soaking into my underwear.

"Great, your gallon of cum makes me look like I've pissed myself."

Stifling a laugh with a cough, Ryan takes my hand and leads me out of the gym to the kitchen.

Every time I enter this kitchen, I am blown away at how gorgeous it is. Sleek metal appliances with a mix of wooden cupboards and solid marble worktops, looks more like a professional kitchen than it does one you'd have in a domestic setting. I'm handed a large glass of apple juice, taking a huge swig, the sharp tangy flavours hit my dry mouth, hydrating me instantly.

"God! This juice is amazing. Where did you get it?"

"It is a juice made from our own trees by the cabin we took you to a while back, we freeze it in batches and when we want some take a load of it out and put it in a jug in the fridge so we can have it all year round, I'm glad it's to your taste."

I down the remaining juice in two large glugs, and smile.

"Ryan, it's delicious, shall I go see Max, now?"

"Leave him to nurse his headache and his wounded pride, he will be right as rain tomorrow."

I nod, understanding where Ryan is coming from.

"I'm gonna ring Luke to check-in, he's probably worried."

"Of course, why not invite him over?"

"That would be amazing, thank you."

I walk away and go into the lounge to make my call.

Ring-Ring

"Hello, tubs, you okay?"

"Hey, you're still in the land of the living then?"

"Yes, you pain in the arse, I have a question for you."

"Yes?"

"Wanna come over for drinks and chats tonight?"

"Are you pulling my leg? Of course, any excuse to come be nosy at your humble abode."

I chuckle and rattle off the address and tell him I'll see him soon.

Chapter Thirteen

Luke arrives about half an hour later and is greeted by Charles and me.

"Bloody hell, even got your own butler."

"Come in, you doughnut."

He steps into the grand entrance hall, looking around in awe.

"Landed on your feet here, eh girl?"

"Yes I have, come on, we will go out to the patio and have some drinks, you still like the old rum, you dirty pirate?"

"Yeah, you got anything good?"

I shake my head and lead him outside to the patio. Waiting for us at the table are two large glasses of rum and cola.

I don't remember asking anyone for it. Weird.

"Staff, to please your every whim, eh, Delaney?"

Luke teases.

I take a long drink, enjoying the spiced flavours.

"Yeah, you cheeky fuck, its taking me a while to get used to it."

We sit and talk for hours getting drunker as the day wears on, laughing, joking like we always have. As it gets dark, Luke announces he should get back as he has work tomorrow.

"Jeez, you're gonna have a rough head tomorrow, I think we went through a whole bottle between us," I say.

As I stand, the effects of the alcohol hit me like a freight train and I sway side to side.

"Me? I think you are gonna be hungover for a week."

He gives me a tight hug making me promise that we will see each other soon and he leaves.

I walk back inside holding the walls and door frames for support and head upstairs, having to crawl up them so I don't lose my balance when it hits me, I should dress up for the guys.

Stupid alcohol addled brain.

I get to my room and find the sexiest outfit I can and try hopelessly to get into the strappy, lacy bodysuit, when I finally get it on I put a dressing gown on (the sort you see in movies of women that have just murdered their husbands, the ones with the fur trim) and go in search for my men. I see Jemma at the end of the hall and wander up to her not caring about how little I am wearing.

"Jemma, do you know where the guys are?"

She looks up at me and her eyes bulge out of her head at the state of me.

"Oh, yes, Ma'am, Mr Matthews is in his study and Mr Romano is in his bedroom."

I walk away proud of my plan and go in search of Ryan.

I knock clumsily at the door and hear a loud, "Enter."

I fumble with the door handle and trip through the door, giggling at my cunning idea.

"What the fuck, Annette?"

He rushes over to me and steadies me.

"Go and sit at your desk. You're ruining my plan," I slur.

Looking amused, he walks back to his large mahogany desk and takes his seat again, I wander over trying to look as sexy as I can in my inebriated state. The laughter in his eyes makes the blueness sparkle. I push him away from the desk so I can get between him and it and remove the dressing gown and perch somewhat elegantly on the edge. Hunger quickly overtakes the laughter in his eyes.

"Fuck, this is a way to interrupt me."

He pushes my legs apart and wheels himself towards me. Grabbing my hips, he scoots me forward so the tiniest amount of my ass is on the desk and rips a hole into the crotch of the bodysuit, making me squeal and giggle.

"What is it with you and tearing my clothes?"

"You just awaken it in me."

He lowers his head and laps at my soft pink lips.

Knock-Knock

"I swear to fucking God everyone has to stop me getting my dick wet."

He whispers to himself.

"What?"

The door swings open to a sleepy-looking Max.

"Hey, no fair, I wanna join."

"Get in here, then, you lumbering oaf, because I swear my balls are gonna burst soon."

I smile at Max and he hurries into the office and stands on the other side of the desk, I turn around so I am facing him with my ass and pussy towards Ryan. Max returns my smile while pulling his already hard dick out of his trousers and brings my head down to it, I lick the tip softly making it twitch and getting rewarded with a groan.

Ryan licks my slit firmly, causing me to lurch forward and take Max's cock deeper into my mouth.

"Annette, you are so responsive to our touch."

Max grabs my hair and starts fucking my mouth roughly but not hard enough to cause me to gag. I hear a belt being undone, then zip and Ryan pushes slowly into my entrance sighing contentedly. My moan at the feeling spurs Max on, Ryan picks up his pace and I am now trapped between my Gods like men. Playing my body like their own instrument makes me cum, my juices dripping onto Ryan's desk as the sounds of our colliding bodies makes the room echo with the sounds.

My men cum inside me with almost perfect timing of each other. Ryan pulls out of me, his cum splatters onto his desk covering what I hope isn't important papers, both men do up their trousers.

"Annie should interrupt you more often, eh, Ry?"

"Definitely."

Ryan helps me off his desk and sits back on his chair.

"Now, both of you go to your own rooms and rest. Annette I can smell the alcohol on you so have some water before you go to sleep, I have to clean up here then I will go to bed myself. We have a busy day tomorrow with lots of meetings."

Max and I leave Ryan to it and go upstairs, Max walks me to my room and gives me a long, passionate goodnight kiss before going to his room. I ignore Ryan's advice and collapse onto my bed, falling straight into a deep sleep.

When I wake the following morning, of course, my head feels like it's been chucked into a cement mixer. I look over to my bedside and find a glass of apple juice with two pills next to it and a note which reads.

A nice glass of juice and some painkillers as I know you won't have listened to my advice. When you feel more human, meet me at work.

Chuckling to myself, I take the tablets and drink the whole drink in three gulps, my body enjoying the much-needed hydration. I amble slowly to the massive en-suite and have a scorchingly hot shower to wake me up. Once washed and dry, I get my clothes out for the day. I decide on a knee-length summer dress which is scarlet red like my hair and some ballet flats. Giving up trying to tame my hair, I scrape it back into a tight ponytail and go light on the make-up and head out for work.

I arrive at work and take my place at my desk and set up my computer for the day ahead.

Ding-Ding

An email notification hits my screen and I read it bleary-eyed from my hangover.

Miss Delaney, now that you have graced the building with your presence, I am having flashbacks at my desk from last night, I hope you are, too. Please fill out the form attached as I need it back ASAP. Hope the hangover doesn't hinder you too much.

Rolling my eyes, I open the form and begin to fill it out, all usual form shite, name, telephone number, etc. When I get to the address I am stumped so I go into Ryan's office and ask, "Ryan, what do I put as my address, your house or mine?"

"I've told you before, sweetheart, that is our home, your old address is waiting till you are ready to sell it."

"Okay, I'll put my new address, thank you, Ryan."

I go back to my desk and continue the form.

When was the last time you had a doctor's check-up?

Fucking strange question.

I cannot remember, so I leave it blank. I finish the form and send it back to Ryan.

Ding-Ding, that didn't take long for a response.

I open the notification and find it's from Max.

Hi, Annie, can you meet me in the lobby? I'm taking you to brunch, it's not fair the mogul gets you there all day, I miss you. I'll be there in ten.

I wave to Ryan as I head to the staff toilets to freshen up, by splashing cool water on my neck from the sink and drying it with a paper towel. Then I go and meet Max at the building's main entrance.

Chapter Fourteen

Sitting in a stupidly fancy restaurant for only brunch, I feel seriously underdressed in my simple dress, I keep eyeing Max who seems to be buzzing with excitement.

"Will you sit still? You're like a child on fucking red bull." I scold him.

"Nope."

I sigh and enjoy my smoked salmon with eggs Benedict, sipping mimosas.

What's a bit more alcohol in my system.

Max is watching me like a hawk now, making me shift uncomfortably in my seat.

"What is your problem, today?" I snap at him.

"Hurry up and finish your food. I wanna take you somewhere."

I eat my food more quickly, confused why my usually big bulky man is acting so oddly. When I have finished, he pays quickly and practically drags me outside and down the street to a little park.

He slows down a little when we get to the park and walks me down a little side path to a wooden gazebo overlooking a little duck pond. We sit down on the steps of it, I try and make sure my dress isn't flashing any unsuspecting passers-by and Max starts to look seriously nervous.

"Are you okay?"

"Who, me? I'm fine."

His phone starts trilling loudly and he wanders off to take the call.

This day gets weirder and weirder.

He saunters back looking proud of himself, while leading a jet-black Friesian horse.

"Max, the horse is beautiful, but I can't ride wearing this."

"That's fine. Come and say hello to your new horse, this is Midnight. She is a gift from Ryan and I."

"Max! You and Ryan shouldn't have, she looks like she cost a fortune."

"She did, but we don't mind, you're worth it."

Clambering up, I jog to my new beastie and give her cuddles and kisses, I feel a lump under her mane and reach under and find a satin ribbon, attached at one end is a plush velvet box. Pulling it out, I stare at Max rather confused at his grinning face.

"What is this?"

"Just open it, you infuriating woman."

Carefully opening it, nestled inside is the most beautiful ring I have ever seen. It is a silver metal ring, which is forged to look like delicate vines intertwined to make the band and there is a massive ruby as the largest stone and its surrounded by smaller diamonds in a circle. The ruby is a beautifully cut stone. When the sunlight hits it, it shines like a tiny fire.

I look up for Max and he isn't there, I feel a tap on my shoulder and I turn to face him and he's kneeling on the ground.

"Miss Delaney, since I met you, you have certainly made my life interesting, to say the least, I never thought in a million years I would find such perfect blissful happiness, I would love to have many more years of it, will you do me the honour of becoming my wife?"

I look down at him shocked.

"What about Ryan and our throuple?"

"You will have to gain some patience and wait and see later, but please answer the damned question, my knee aches."

I nod franticly with tears in my eyes.

"Yes, you blithering idiot, yes."

He shoots up, making Midnight shake her head, and hug me so tightly my feet lift off the ground. He slides the ring onto my ring finger, beaming like a child on Christmas day.

Charles appears out of nowhere and leads Midnight off.

"Charles is going to take her to the stables at the cabin for us and we can visit this weekend."

I smile at him, over the moon at how the day has turned out but still concerned about how Ryan fits in with all of this.

We walk to Max's car and he opens the passenger door and helps me into it.

"Am I not going back to work?"

"Nope, I am taking you home for the next surprise."

We drive in silence for a while and I just stare at my beautiful ring, admiring the intricate work that makes up the strands of the band.

"You do like it, right? It reminded us of you, fiery and unique."

"Yes, Max, I love it. You two couldn't have picked a more perfect ring."

Smiling to himself, he pulls onto the long driveway that enters the land surrounding our home, he parks at the bottom of the steps at the front of the house and says, "Go on into the lounge for your next surprise, I will join you, soon."

Taking the steps two at a time, I race into the lounge to be greeted by thousands of beautiful flowers, the scent is amazing. Sat in the middle of them on the floor on a blanket is my second man.

"Annette, please come sit beside me."

I do as I am told, looking around our transformed living room in awe.

"Now, I know Max has done his speaking from the heart and has proposed, I am not very good at expressing myself, but for you, I shall try. Since you came to my office on the first day, I knew you were going to be a force to be reckoned with, even with your shirt undone."

I laugh at the memory.

"Now, I have a gift as well."

He hands me a large jewellery box and I tentatively open it, inside is a pair of earrings and a necklace that match my beautiful engagement ring.

"Wow, Ryan these are beautiful."

"Now, legally, you can only be married to one of us so on paper. You will be married to me, but we will do a special service for all three of us to show our love to friends and family, the reason for the form earlier was to make us your next of kin and you ours, so if anything should happen, we are safe legally and you are protected."

I nod, trying to take all this information in.

"Max represents the ring and I the other jewellery."

"Thank you so, so much."

Max strolls into the lounge.

"What did she say, then?"

"Maximus, you are very good at arriving prematurely, she hasn't answered yet."

"Yes, of course, yes I love you both dearly. You complement me and my personality perfectly, like pieces I didn't know I was missing."

"Good, because Frankie is getting impatient." Max tuts.

"Come on then, we can't make the artiste wait," Ryan says rolling his eyes.

We walk out to the garden where I learn Frankie is an overzealous, very, very flamboyant, French-accented photographer who the guys employed to take our official engagement photos.

"'Ere comes ze beautiful swan who has taken zees hunky men off the market. There will be tears when zees photos are released to ze public."

I laugh at his expression. We spend the whole afternoon taking pictures and I laugh so hard by the time we finish, my sides are aching. The photos that we have are stunning and Frankie promises to write a beautiful article for the local magazine to accompany them for tomorrow's issue. He leaves and my men and I have a relaxing evening with films and champagne.

Chapter Fifteen

The next few days go by so fast, they make my head spin, doing interviews with my men for magazines and lots of shopping, as my men said if I am going to be their wife they want me to have lots of clothes. Ryan at one point said he was going to build me a walk-in wardrobe.

Still not convinced he isn't.

On Friday, we head to the cabin for much needed R&R, I ache all over from the miles walked over this week. I went into a few shops while the guys weren't looking and brought some surprises for the guys this weekend.

Can't wait to see their faces at the skimpy lingerie.

We arrive just as the sun begins to set and Max says, "No riding Midnight without one of us with you, there is a lot of farmers around here that shoot first and ask questions later when it comes to people on their land, and you're not overly familiar with the area."

I nod and head inside, excited to strip off for my men as we haven't had time for sex really this week.

Sprinting upstairs, I lock myself into the bathroom and get into one of the sets, praying they like the overpriced lace. The lingerie itself is beautiful, satin bodice with overly intricate lace and a matching G-string, it is a mix of red and black. Two colours which, to me, symbolise passion. I look in the mirror and wince.

What if they don't like it?

I put stupidly high heels on my feet and teeter downstairs in search of my hopefully surprised men. Max is in the lounge trying to light the fire to heat the cabin and Ryan is overseeing, taking the piss every time the match goes out.

"Thought being the son of a big mafia boss meant you had some survival skills like making a fucking fire?"

Max spins on Ryan, obviously going to give him a few choice words, but his eyes land on me in the doorframe, noticing Max isn't looking at him Ryan turns and his mouth flops open. I look down at my feet, not knowing how I feel about the men's stares.

"Don't you like it? I can go change."

I go to turn away.

"NO!" they shout in unison and run towards me, Max grabs my waist and pulls me in for teeth clashing kiss, Ryan steps behind me and starts kissing my neck, nipping periodically, making my skin tingle and my body come alive.

They both caress my outfit, feeling the soft lace, grumbling in appreciation.

"I don't remember you getting this," Ryan says curiously.

"That's because I brought it as a surprise for you two among other outfits as you two have been so kind buying me enough clothes to open a shop, I thought I'd repay you with these."

Max jolts upright.

"There're more outfits?"

I nod my head and Max looks gobsmacked.

"I wanna see so bad. Can you show us, please?"

"Yeah, I mean you can, but there is no definite they are gonna look good."

"On you, they will, sweetheart," Ryan mumbles into my neck.

So the remaining few hours of the day is spent with me having my own fashion show to my two men. No I didn't get my sex sadly, we all fell asleep in front of the fire, Max finally got to the light.

The following morning, I wake before the guys and go for a walk to the stables and spend some time with Midnight, brushing and braiding her mane and tail, while chatting about what wedding I want, and how I'm going to learn to ride properly, so I can ride her into the ceremony side saddle so I can be elegant for once in my life.

"That's good, then, there is a riding coach coming in about an hour. Ryan and I thought it would be best you learnt to do more than walk and turn as Midnight here would go to waste."

Max's voice comes from outside the stable door.

"How much of my conversation did you eavesdrop on?"

"Enough to know how to help you plan our wedding."

"Oh, no."

"Oh, yes, now go get ready for your lesson."

An hour later, I'm at Midnight cursing myself for not having a sports bra, my tits are bouncing like fucking Tiger on a sugar rush. I get the hang of trot within half an hour. Max looks very proud of me.

"That's enough for today, as much as I love watching your boobs bounce, you are going to ache tomorrow already, and I don't want to put you off just yet."

He pays the man and the man leaves, I walk Midnight back to the stable and Max takes her tack off and leads her to the field to roam around.

We walk back to the cabin, Max laughing at me as I am waddling from being saddle sore.

"Don't take the piss."

"But it is so funny."

Hearing Max's laughter, Ryan meets us on the porch looking bemused, he notices my walking and joins in.

"You two are arseholes."

That only fuels their laughter. Wincing with every step, I make my way indoors and go and have a hot shower to soothe my aching muscles. I take the time and wash my hair, enjoying the heat of the water on my body. Grabbing a towel, I slowly dry myself before moisturising with my favourite body lotion which makes me smell like a florist.

When I finally emerge from my room, the smell of spices being cooked drifts up the stairs, following my nose to the kitchen; my stomach grumbles loudly.

"Hungry are we, John Wayne?"

"Yes I am, when are you two gonna finish taking the Mick out of me?"

"Not for a while Annette, you did look funny walking like you had peed yourself."

Ryan is cooking what looks like a stir-fry which smells amazing.

We sit and eat in comfortable silence enjoying our meal, when we are finished, the boys send me out onto the veranda to have a cigarette while they tidy up after dinner.

I love these men, I hardly ever have to wash up, which is one of my least favourite jobs to do.

I sit outside enjoying the cool air, gazing up at the beautiful sky and the twinkling stars.

I should probably ring my mother for our monthly call soon. My mother and I have a love-hate relationship.

I pull out my phone and dial my mother.
"Hi, mum, just checking in how are you?"
"Still in the land of the living."

Shame.

"Have you been busy, mum? How is the garden coming along?"
"Yes, I've been busy, do you have anything else to say? I am late to meet your cousin at the pub."

Ever so chatty, my mother loves a good drink.

"Okay, mum, speak soon, bye."
Before I have said my goodbyes, she hangs up.
"Well, bye to you, too, you ungrateful wench."

"You okay, Annie?"
Max looks concerned and worried.
"I'm fine, just spoke to my mother."
"You never mention her, do you not get on?"
"My mother and I tolerate each other, and make sure the other is breathing."
"Oh, that good, then."
"Yup."

He pulls me into his arms and holds me tightly to him, he takes my cigarette and has a puff before handing it back. We sit for a while in silence looking up at the night sky.

"Annie? What kind of wedding do you want?"

"Small and intimate, but full of personal touches."

"Sounds like a plan to me."

We discuss wedding details till Ryan comes out in a fluster.

"Debra, the wedding planner I've organised to help you, said she's only got one space this year and that is in three months, I know that is a bit of a quick engagement, but the next appointment with her isn't for two years."

"Ryan, relax, I would marry you tomorrow if I could, now tell me Debra's number and I will go start planning, I'm so excited!"

He rattles off the number and I go inside.

Ring-Ring

"Debra speaking, how may I help you?"

"Hello, I am Annette Delaney. Ryan Matthews said to give you a call about wedding preparations?"

"Yes, of course, Ma'am."

Since being with my men, a lot of people now call me Ma'am.

"We would like something small and full of personal touches."

"Yes, of course, are you free tomorrow? I could come by and show you some swatches of colour schemes and things like that. Mr Matthews has told me about your unique ceremony requirements, such as two lucky grooms."

"That will be perfect. And I have one thing I really want to do and that is riding my horse Midnight to the ceremony, but that will be difficult with a dress, won't it?"

"Have no fear. We will find a way. Goodbye, Miss Delaney."

"Goodbye."

Chapter Sixteen

Debra arrives promptly in the morning carrying huge folders filled with wedding ideas. We sort through different ideas from flowers, to where the wedding will be held. I decide on baby breaths with lavender, white roses and lilies for my bouquet and white roses for buttonholes. The centrepieces for the tables will match my bouquet. I decided we should have the wedding in a local medieval barn. I have seen pictures of weddings there and they look beautiful, the beams covered in soft twinkly lights and it feels very magical like a fairy-tale. I pick pale purple and white as a colour scheme. Debra is very excited as she has never done a polyamorous wedding before. I didn't realise Max and Ryan getting married would be such big news as the wedding planner slips out that this will be one of the biggest marriages this decade.

Ryan pokes his head around the door.

"Don't forget to include our security, the tech team will go in first to set up surveillance cameras before people start arriving."

I look over at him, confused.

"When did we get security?"

"Sweetheart, you have always had it while we have been together, they were just told to be discreet, as not to alarm you."

"What the fuck you had people watching me and didn't think to tell me?"

"It was, so you didn't feel uncomfortable."

"They obviously don't do a good job, I've been kidnapped twice."

Ignoring Debra's shocked face, Ryan replies matter-of-factly.

"And they were fired for it, the first time the man watching your house nipped away to relieve himself and when he came back you are taken. Then he was saving his own ass and didn't contact us while we were in Sicily to let us know. The second time you were too quick for your security, and again they were fired."

I look at him gobsmacked.

"Jesus, Mary and Joseph, you should have told me, but I understand why you didn't, now piss off so I can organise my dream wedding."

He stares at the woman opposite me, making her look extremely worried.

"Anything she wants, she gets, money is no object."

"Y-yes sir, of course."

Ryan storms off, leaving us to sort everything out.

"Sorry about him, he's a miserable prick."

She laughs, but makes her excuses to leave, promising to bring me an idea board of everything in a few days.

I walk her out to her car and wave her off. Ryan is my next port of call to teach him some manners. Finding him in the gym working on the punching bag, I sneak up behind him and try to kick his legs out, he spins grunting in pain, as his head turns, I lift my fist and hit him in the jaw.

"Ouch, what the fuck?"

He grumbles rubbing his chin.

"You need to learn some manners, you terrified the poor woman."

"She had to know the budget."

I take a few swings to the bag, slowly getting into a steady rhythm.

Thud-Thud-Thud

"Annette, I'm sorry I was rude to the lady. Will you talk to me about what was discussed yet?"

Thud-Thud-Thud

I'm in a trance-like state hitting, kicking and giving the bag all I've got. Sweat beads at my forehead, my body enjoying the burn in my muscles as they work hard to alleviate my frustration. Ryan grabs me and pulls me away.

"Annette, enough! You're going too hard, you are going to hurt yourself."

That is enough to bring me out of the spell.

"What the hell, Ryan! I was focused like you've told me to be when we spar."

"Yes, but that's training for life and death situations and you were blank-faced and not hearing me, is everything okay? Is something on your mind?"

"I'm worried about planning the wedding when Giovanni is still out there, I don't want anything to ruin the big day."

Ryan walks over to the other side of the room and returns with a purple velvet bag.

Handing it to me, he whispers.

"Open it."

Inside the bag is a well-decorated silver dagger in a sheath, there are straps on the sheath make it able to be worn on the thigh discretely.

"Wear that and you will feel a little more comfortable, Max will teach you to use it effectively whether he likes it or not, Max is very skilled with all sized blades."

Bending down, Ryan attaches it to my thigh with adept fingers making sure it's not too tight.

"Thank you, Ryan, I apologise for being so stressful."

"It's fine, come on, we have to persuade 'Maxy' to teach you to use blade."

"No, I don't care what Ryan said. I am not teaching you how to weld a blade, you are way too clumsy, you will end up hurting yourself or me in the process of training."

"Max, what about if I get kidnapped again because of your incompetent security team? Would you rather I die?" I try to blackmail him.

"Fine. One hour, that's it, just enough to learn some basic moves, you little blackmailer."

"Thank you, thank you, thank you! Max, why are you so against teaching me?"

"When I was a child, the padre made my mother train every day to be able to protect herself, and he controlled what she ate and when. In the end, she ended up dying of a cross between malnutrition and exhaustion as she overworked herself."

Max looks heartbroken talking about his mother, they must have had a close bond.

"I'm sorry, Max, that must have been horrible."

"It really was. I found her laying on the floor of the gym with glassy eyes and a blank expression. My father couldn't care less. He was remarried in a month to his young leggy secretary, who happens to be Giovanni's mother."

"I'm not sad that the padre is dead, he was a creepy man and apparently, a cunt, too."

Max chuckles softly.

"Come on, little warrior, let's get started, I have some wooden blades to practice with."

For the next hour and a half, Max slowly takes me through some basic moves to injure an opponent with the least amount of force. I practice switching hands while he tries to wrestle me and I accidentally time it wrong and hit him in the nose with the hilt and it begins to bleed.

"Ouch, I guess that's a cue to leave the training there, you can practice those moves over and over to make sure you are ready for a surprise attack."

"I'm so sorry, Max, are you okay?"

He nods then pinches his nose to stem the bleeding.

Crash-Bang-Crash

Ryan comes sprinting into the gym and shouts at us.

"Annette, go hide. Max, come with me! Charles's body has just been found on the front doorstep with his intestines pulled out of his body, there is blood everywhere and I've told Jemma and the rest of the female staff to go hide, the security team are on high alert. GO, NOW! Annette, my office is probably the best place, lock the door behind you and hide under the desk."

Tears streaming down my face, I run to the office and hide under the desk sobbing quietly, I hope my men are safe. I hear the security team run past, barking orders at one another.

My phone vibrates and an unknown number flashes up a text notification.

Dear darling little pet. Your keeper's butler was just a warning that I haven't forgotten you, don't worry my dear, I will have you soon.

It's Giovanni, he killed Charles because of me. I sob louder and Max comes barging into the room.

"Whoever it was they escaped, went through a hole in the fence, we have two armed guards there now to make sure he doesn't come back."

"Max, did Charles have any family?"

"Only us lot, that's why he was a good hire, but Jesus he put up a fight, his knuckles were split from him punching whoever it was."

I can't tell them it was Giovanni, I can't tell them. He will try and take them out if they try to fight him.

I nod and Max leads me out of the office and upstairs into my room.

"We need to have a funeral for Charles," I whisper.

"We will, Annie, just tonight get some sleep. Ry and I will be joining you soon."

I numbly get undressed, shower and get into bed. Sleep evades me as I toss and turn, trying to get comfortable to sleep, but the thought of Charles and my kidnappings plague my mind.

Max and Ryan join me after two in the morning, they hold either side of me and pass out cold. They are so exhausted that they don't notice I am still awake. I finally crash into a fitful sleep at about 6 a.m. when the light starts to come through the curtains. I sleep for maybe two hours, waking with an awful headache. The first thing I notice is I am alone in my bed and it is cold, so my men didn't get much sleep either. Dragging my lazy arse out of bed I get into the shower to freshen myself up, I let the warm water run down my shoulders and close my eyes, sighing momentarily, forgetting how fucked up everything is in my life right now. Alas, it doesn't last long and I exit the shower, ready to face reality and bury one of my lovers' employees. We are burying him quickly so the authorities don't ask any awkward questions. Dressing in a simple black shift dress and black stilettos, I make my way downstairs and to my men who are both dressed in immaculately tailored suits that hug their bodies in a way that if this wasn't a funeral I'd be taking them upstairs to fuck me till my throat was hoarse. We head off in a motorcade of cars, some cars with security, some with household staff wishing to say goodbye to their beloved friend. I sit in a car with Max and Ryan with two guards upfront.

"We will get our revenge, don't worry, sweetheart. Max and I are trying to find the culprit. The tech team are trailing through the surveillance as we speak."

I nod sadly and look to my feet. We arrive at the humongous church and the heavens open, Ryan gets out and grabs an umbrella from the boot and we all walk up to the church and take our places inside. Lining every wall is men in black suits armed to the hilt and wearing earpieces. The motorcade outside is waiting for people to slowly file into the church and take their seats. There are probably thirty or so people in the church excluding security. The funeral begins and the coffin is brought in, the sight of the coffin makes my eyes well up and Max puts his arm around me to support me.

The service was beautiful and very simple. Charles was buried in the churchyard as his will stated, we head home and have a long soak in the bath, to warm up from the cold. Outside it is dark and thundery. During the night we have several power cuts, the lightning illuminates the darkened house with quick flashes. We curl up under my duvet as I don't like storms and hold each other tightly.

Chapter Seventeen

"Fucking, Ryan!"

I have awoken to a note saying I'm fired because I am to be Ryan and Max's wife soon, so I cannot work for the company as it will be shown as favouritism by the other staff, but I don't have to look for another job right away as the boys like me being home and safe.

Fucking safe, my arse! I was kidnapped from here once, I know my sulky toddlers have tripled the security, but I love being useful and doing stuff.

I go about my day, pouting about the letter, but I don't message either of my men to make them sweat a bit. I keep busy by finalising wedding details and punching the ever-loving crap out of the punch bag to keep my emotions in check. At lunchtime, I go down to the underground garage and decide to mess with the stupidly expensive, noisy cars. I open all the petrol caps and pull all the windscreen wipers out and I hide all the keys.

Fucking mess with me boys, I'll get you back.

I sit at the dining table eating a bowl of freshly made macaroni and cheese when Ryan gets back from work looking rather red-faced.

"What have you done to my collection of vintage cars?"

"What have you done with my job?"

I counter, feeling very clever.

"I said you could get another."

"BUT! You fired me. I love working there."

"I know. Can I have the keys back now?"

"Yes, of course, they are in a bag in the middle of the pool. Splash, splash, enjoy your swim."

Ryan stalks over to me and pulls me up out of my seat and throws me over his shoulder.

"It's only fair you enjoy a swim, too."

"Ry, what the hell are you doing with her?"

"Ah, Max, I am teaching our beautiful woman a lesson."

"What's she done now?"

"Well, my classic car keys are in the pool because we fired her."

"I have got to see this."

Squealing as Ryan walks, I try to escape his grasp with no luck, and he hands his phone and wallet to Max and steps into the pool, I surface coughing and laughing, my makeup dripping down my face.

"You prick, Ryan Matthews," I say only half-joking.

"I know I am, Miss Delaney, but on this occasion, you started it."

Max is laid on the floor pissing himself laughing, so I swim up to him and splash him, which makes him curse in surprise.

I clamber out of the swimming pool looking like a drowned rat. Both men find this hilarious.

Plop, slap. Plop, slap

The sound of me walking through the house even makes me chuckle to myself.

Ring-Ring

I answer my phone cautiously.

"Annette, it's Debra. I have organised a dress boutique to open for you this afternoon so you can have a private fitting all to yourself."

"Thank you so much. What time will I need to be there?"

"The appointment is for 3 p.m. I will meet you there."

"Thank you so much for this. With everything going on, I haven't had a chance to organise a dress."

"You are most welcome. I'll see you later."

I arrive at the boutique, greet Debra and the shop owner, and then begin to try on beautiful dresses. The first is form-fitting and I look into the mirror and it makes me look like a knock off mermaid. The second is a lace 1950s style. One that makes me look beautiful, but it's not 'the one', so I put it aside for later. The third is the perfect fairy-tale dress, a white satin corset with lace flowers over it. The skirt is a floor-length, poofy skirt that I try on and feel like a princess, I match it with white satin shoes and a handmade veil that has a stunning hand-stitched scalloped hem with pearls dangling off the edge. I twirl around and Debra giggles and takes lots of photos for the wedding album.

"That is the perfect one, you look like a Disney princess."

I turn to the shop owner.

"Please, I will take these."

I pay and make arrangements to have the final fittings, and head down the street to a small coffee shop for a drink. Inside, I say hello to Katy who works there.

"How are you, Katy? May I have a pot of tea and a blueberry muffin, please?"

"Of course, take your usual seat out the front in the sunshine."

"Thank you so much."

I pay, then go sit in the sunshine and have a cigarette while I wait. Katy brings out my tea and sits in the chair opposite.

"Annie, can I nab a cigarette? I'm craving so bad."

I hand her one over, followed by a lighter.

I drink my tea slowly, chatting to my old school friend.

"Katy, I cannot wait for your wedding cake, it's sure to be amazing."

"Annie, I'm proud you asked me, can't believe my little shop is going to be in a magazine."

"I better be off, but I will see you soon."

I give her a massive hug and drive home.

I arrive home to a very worried Ryan and Max.

"Where did you go, Annette? We have been worried sick. The tech guys saw your car leave the drive and told us. We have been trying to ring you all afternoon." Ryan chastises me.

"I'm sorry. I forgot to tell you Debra rang and asked me to go see her."

"Jesus, Annie, do you want us to have a heart attack before we get married? You should not have gone off without anyone, the guards did not even notice till the tech guy saw the camera, Ryan has been blowing up at them for ages."

I look down guiltily.

"I can't have Giovanni rule what I can and can't do, it will make me stir crazy."

"WE CAN'T HAVE YOU DEAD EITHER!"

Ryan roars at me. I look at him with worried eyes.

"Ryan, I know. I just can't live in fear because of him."

"It won't be long and our guys will track him down, they will tear him limb from limb for what he did to you."

I nod, feeling a little better with the information that the slimy snake is being watched, even if he seems to slip through the cracks if he so chooses.

We all head up to what will be the master bedroom and the guys start to undress me, Max kisses my bare shoulder making me shiver with wanton desire. Ryan goes into the en-suite and turns on the massive shower. The walls and the floor is made from light granite and in the ceiling are three, black squared showerheads that are pumping out steaming water. We all enter the shower and Max begins to knead soap into my back and neck, causing a blissful sigh to leave me. Ryan then kneels and laps the water dripping down between my thighs, catching my clit with the faintest of touches, my hips buck in response. Both men work down my body till Max is squeezing and slapping my arse and Ryan's tongue is thrusting in and out of my pussy. My body quakes with the onslaught of touch, Max holds my waist to keep me still, while his teeth graze my ass cheeks.

Ryan shifts and pushes his long dextrous finger into my pussy, replacing his tongue. I lean my head back, enjoying my men worshipping my body.

Max traces my other puckered entrance with his finger, causing me to gasp at the new sensation.

"Can you take me back here?" Max whispers softly.

"Fuck, yes." I moan, almost desperate.

Max gently pushes his finger slowly inside my ass, causing an elongated moan to erupt from my mouth. Having both men's fingers inside me gives me a satisfyingly full feeling.

"I wonder what it will be like to have both of your cocks inside me."

Ryan chuckles.

"Your wish is our command."

Ryan withdraws from my body and Max follows suit. Lifting me, Ryan positions me onto his cock and holds me still while Max lines himself up at my back entrance, with one smooth stroke he fills me completely.

"Fucking hell!"

"You okay? Annie, is it too much?"

I whimper softly. "Let me get used to it for a moment."

The men were still, allowing me to adjust.

"Move now, please."

They both move in sync, making my body clench in delicious ways. They build up the pace till the both of them are grunting hard and making me scream their names as I cum time after time till my body is exhausted, both the men orgasm together filling me with their intoxicating cum.

I cannot get enough of these men.

They pull out of my body and Ryan lowers me down to the shower floor and helps me rinse off our amorous activities from my body.

Dried and dressed, we lay on the bed, Max snoring like rocks in a blender, Ryan and I take turns in asking each other questions.

"Ryan, what are your parents like?"

"Well, my mother is a very kind and caring woman who has blonde, wavy hair and beautiful blue eyes like me, and my father was a business associate of the padre, so you can imagine what kind of man he is. He regularly hurts my mother, which drives me insane as I cannot do anything about it because my mother won't allow me to hurt the bastard. She tells me it's the alcohol, not him that hurts her."

"I would love to meet her. I'm sorry you have had to watch your father be cruel to her."

"Annette, Max said you do not like your mother, so what is your father like?"

"That man is a sperm donor and nothing more, he hasn't been in my life since I was born and I've never tried to contact him, he's the kinda man that likes to put it about."

"That's fair enough, he is missing out massively though." I shrug and snuggle closer to him.

"Ryan, how did you and Max meet?"

"We met at a mafia family function, one where out the front is all the families having a party and out the back dodgy deals happen. Max and I were skimming stones across the padre's fishing lake and got told off by security when we smashed an ornament."

"I bet you were right little rascals when you were kids."

"Yes, we were. One night, we stole two guest mattresses from my parents' house and used them as rafts in the indoor pool."

I giggle at the images of two young boys being scolded for their misbehaviour.

"Annette, it is my turn to ask. Have you ever imagined yourself a mother?"

"Yes, but I do not know how it would work with us three."

"Sweetheart, if you fell pregnant, we will raise the child together."

I smile and kiss him softly and yawn loudly.

"Sleep, Annette, we all need our rest as we get married in two weeks and you need to make sure you are rested up for the honeymoon."

He smiles with a twinkle in his eyes.

I lay my head down on his chest and drift into the first deep, refreshing sleep I have had in weeks.

Chapter Eighteen

The following morning, I wake up to my two men snoring loudly in my ears. I cover my ears and chuckle to myself. Padding downstairs, I go in search of breakfast. I decide on pancakes with fruit. I put some music on and dance about while I cook. Just as I'm dishing up, the guys announce their presence by coughing aloud, I look up and two pairs of eyes are gazing at me, looking very entertained at my dancing.

"Breakfast is served. Hope they are okay."

Not even taking a breath, the pancakes are devoured within minutes.

"Did you two even chew or breathe?"

"Annie, they were lovely. Maybe you can teach us the recipe?"

"Nope, no way. I want to be able to do something for you two."

"You do, Annie. You make us cum like fountains."

I throw a tea towel at him, which make him nearly fall off his chair with laughter.

"Don't be so bloody crude, now you two can go wash up."

I look ever so innocently at them, knowing that I am a terrible mess when I cook.

Swimming laps to work some of the huge stacks of pancakes, I zone out and think of all that has happened in the last few months from the kidnappings and meeting the men I am going to marry, I am lucky that I have two men to love me wholly and with their every being. I then start to think of the future and little, dark-haired children running through the gardens. I would like to get a dog for them to play with. I don't think I could get another cat yet. It's too raw. I would like several children. A boy first though, to look after his younger siblings, and I would like them to all do little chores around the house, so they are grounded and know the value of money. I dive deeper into the pool but forget how close I am to the side and bump my head in the process.

Ouch! Fuck, that side is bloody hard.

I pull myself out and sit on the side, a bit dazed. I stand after a while and walk back to the main part of the house.

"Ryan! Max!"

Running over to me, the guys grab me as I sink to the floor.

"Annette! What has happened?"

"I hit my head on the side of the pool and feel a bit woozy."

Max lifts me and walks me to the sofa.

"You are seriously the clumsiest girl I have ever met."

"I am not clumsy. The walls just get in the way, the chairs are bullies and the floors have it out for me."

Both of them chuckle at me and Ryan grabs me an ice pack for my now egg-sized lump at the top of my head.

"I hope this lump goes down in time for the wedding."

"It will, but we have to get you to the hospital to make sure your brains aren't scrambled, Annie."

"Fuck off and let me sleep."

"Ry, go grab the car for Ms stubborn arse. I'll drag her out to it."

"Don't you dare!"

Lifting me as if I weigh as much as paper, Max carries me to the waiting car and puts me in and fastens the seatbelt for me.

Jesus, I feel sick as a dog.

Ryan looks into the rear-view mirror.

"Do not be sick in this car, I have just had it cleaned after the cum incident and it's ten minutes to the hospital. Hold it in."

Managing not to be sick in Ryan's precious car, we arrive at the local accident and emergency and they see me very quickly and decide I need a CT scan. As I am rolled down to the scanner, I begin to feel extremely nauseous again.

"Stop, stop, stop the wheelchair, please."

"Are you okay, Madam?" The poor, nervous-looking porter asks.

I think me having two large men in my room scared him a little.

"No! I feel sick."

He stops the wheelchair and grabs me a sick bucket. I swear to Jesus Mary and Joseph I have never puked so much in all my life. I end up using four sick buckets before my stomach is settled enough to continue to the scanner room. I lay on the CT bed and have the scan. The lady who does it is very patient with me and a credit to the NHS. She is very gentle with my cannula when she pushes some fluid into it and actually comes with me back to my room to explain the results to me and my very worried-looking men.

"Miss Delaney has a mild concussion and should make a speedy recovery, the sickness is just the bump on her head which has just rattled her brain a little."

"She was sick?" Ryan asks.

"Yes, sir, but that is perfectly normal."

"Will this bloody lump go down before our wedding in a couple of weeks?" I ask, now seriously pissed, I wasted everyone's time.

"Yes, it should, who is the lucky man then."

"Both."

I reply, waiting for the shock and immediate disgust.

"Well, they are very fortunate, Miss Delaney, my wife and I tied the knot three months ago."

"Congratulations, and thank you for taking care of our sourpuss."

Max says, sticking his tongue out at me like a bloody child.

"You are most welcome, I will write up the results and the doctor should be in shortly."

I lay down on the white scratchy sheets of the hospital bed and close my eyes.

"Have you had any more letters from my brother dearest?"

Max says, not realising that I am not asleep.

"Yes, I have received one stating that our engagement has not gone over well. I have lost three security guards at the cabin in as many days, he's out for blood. I will be glad when we are all on our honeymoon and can't be traced."

"Are we any closer to finding the mole in our organisation yet?"

"Adam, the new tech guy, has a few suggestions."

"If he is new, how can we trust him?"

"Because his sister was brutally raped and murdered by a bloodthirsty Giovanni when he was very intoxicated."

"How the fuck am I related to such a low life prick?"

"Because your daddy was a manwhore."

Both men chuckle and I open my eyes.

"Annie, shit, how are you feeling?"

"Like I was hit by a bus, can you go grab a nurse and ask for some pain meds please, Max?"

"Of course, I will be right back."

"Ryan, I heard every word that was discussed between you two. We need to step up my training, and I want to gut that evil, disgusting cockroach myself."

"No."

"What do you mean no?"

"I am not putting you in that much danger, you have learnt enough to defend yourself effectively, but that is all either of us are teaching, we cannot lose you."

I sigh angrily at the stupid, over-protective man.

Max strolls in smiling, holding a little paper cup in one hand and what I am hoping is some pain meds. He stops when he notices the tension in the room.

"What the hell is going on between you two?"

"Nothing," I mumble.

"Our beautiful wife-to-be wants to be the one to put Giovanni out of action."

"No, not in a million years, Annie. You may be able to stab or knock him out, but don't doubt, he would probably have a sniper somewhere aimed at you for retaliation."

"I would be fine," I say through gritted teeth.

The doctor chooses that moment to grace us with his presence. He checks me over, taking my blood pressure and checking my heart, his fingers rough and clumsy. Even at one point, he grabs my boob. He straightens up and says, "Miss Delaney, looking at your scans, we would like to keep you in overnight for observation and you can go home tomorrow. I will say now only your boyfriend can stay, your friend cannot."

"Excuse me, doctor, they are both my boyfriends."

The doctor looks at me in shock, underlined with disgust.

"Well, regardless, only one can stay. Hospital policy."

My men look at each other like they are having a silent conversation.

"Max will stay, I will sleep in the car in the car park, so I am nearby."

"Sir," the doctor pipes up. "Wouldn't you rather go home? Staying that long in the car park is expensive."

Ryan strides up to him and stands nose to nose.

"I know you are treating the love of my life so I will try to remain calm, but if it meant I was near her, I would make myself broke."

The doctor loses all the colour on his face.

"Of course, sir, I apologise."

He nods to me and flees the room.

"Ryan Matthews, that wasn't very nice, he's only doing his job."

"He pissed me off and don't think I didn't notice how rough and handsy he was with you, slimy prick, gets off touching up unwell, young women."

I smile and chuckle, Ryan leans down and kisses my lips with a feather-light touch.

"Goodnight ,Annette, I'm only a phone call away if Mr bear's snoring keeps you awake."

"Hey! I do not snore like a bear, I purr like a cat."

"Maxy, sweetheart, you sound like rocks in a blender."

"How bloody rude, you wound me," he says clutching his chest, acting the fool.

Ryan leaves the room, looking very pissed he has to go.

Max sits on the nearby armchair for guests and closes his eyes.

"Maxy, please, lay with me. I do not like hospitals, they make me anxious."

"Annie, you are meant to be resting, and remember, I snore like a bear."

I burst into loud sobs, shaking hard.

"Oh, Annie, don't cry."

He leans over and takes my hand, his thumb stroking the back in soothing circular motions.

"I'm sorry, but I really hate this clinical place."

He stands and kisses my forehead. He removes his jacket and shoes, lifts me gently, causing me to wince as my head pounds at the jostling.

"Annie, sorry, I shouldn't have moved you."

"It is fine, please hold me while I sleep."

Max lays down next to me with my head resting on his chest. I fall asleep within minutes.

"Excuse me, sir, this bed is for hospital patients only."

"I'm sorry, Ma'am, but she is scared of hospitals, so I was holding her to keep her calm."

"Just be sure you're out of the bed before the doctors come round in half an hour."

"Thank you, I will."

The nurse leaves and I lift my head to gaze at my man.

"Thank you for staying with me. When I was a teenager, I became very mentally poor and my mother locked me into a psychiatric unit for two months. I spent the entire time drugged so much that I was like a zombie. One of the doctors who was looking after me took advantage of my intoxicated state and took my innocence from me."

Max looks at me with tears in his eyes.

"Where was that place?"

"It is attached to this hospital, the building at the back."

Max looks full of rage.

"Give me a moment, honey, I need to make a call. What was this man's name?"

"Dr Fitzgerald. What are you going to do?"

"That disgusting excuse of a human being isn't going to hurt anyone else."

Max walks into the bathroom to make his call. I can hear his voice raise several times during it and he comes out looking much calmer.

"Who did you call?"

I question, lifting myself up from the bed to sit up. He hurries over to me and helps me sit up and take a sip of water.

"I spoke to Martin, our head of security and our top hitman."

"What did he say?"

"That the doctor will go missing soon."

His voice sounds lethal.

Knock-Knock

The nurse from earlier enters with my discharge papers.

"No doctor sign off?"

"No, sir. The doctor is happy with Miss Delaney's overnight observations, He is happy for her to go home, but she must rest for three days."

"I can't rest, I am getting married in two weeks."

112

"Annie, we will organise Debra to visit our home so you can rest and recuperate."

"Okay, let's go home then."

Chapter Nineteen

The next few days are absolute hell. Ryan and Max won't even let me walk to the bathroom to pee. They wait outside while I do my business and get me to call when I'm done. I walked to the door of the bathroom and get berated for not being careful. By the third day, I am livid and have cabin fever. Ryan went to the office so Max was babysitting, me but had fallen asleep on the bed, so I snuck out and went to the library at the other end of the house and hid and began to read my favourite book *'Dark Visions'* by L.J Smith. I enjoy the peace and quiet laid on the oversized beanbag. Sitting bolt upright when I hear a throat clear, I see a strange man looking at me from the door, he has short blonde hair and an expression that says he doesn't take shit from anyone.

"Who are you?"

"Madam, my name is Martin, I am the head of security. I am fairly sure you are meant to be on bed rest."

"Technically, I was told to rest, she never specified where. What happened with Dr Fitzgerald?"

"I was told not to enclose any details to you, but I can say that he won't bother anyone else again."

"Did he suffer?"

"Yes, Ma'am."

"Good, I only wish I could have kicked his bollocks."

Martin laughs, "You are tougher than you are given credit for. I think your men are trying to wrap you in cotton wool."

"Does that mean you would train me to fight?"

"Ma'am, I love my job. I will not jeopardise it, but I will say use that pretty little knife you were gifted wherever on the body you can. It will throw off your opponent that a lady such as yourself carries a weapon."

"I will keep that in mind, thank you, Martin. Is Max looking for me, then?" I ask, noticing Martin keeps touching his earpiece.

"Yeah, he's been screaming down the comms."

"Okay, I guess my peace and quiet is broken. Tell him I am here."

Martin relays my message and bids me a good day.

Max is not happy I disappeared on him.

"Annie, I was worried sick. I thought you had been taken again or that I would find you on the doorstep like Charles. do not do that to me again."

Feeling like a scolded child, I nod and look at my feet.

"Sorry, Max, I have hated being stuck in bed. I needed some time out of the same four walls."

"You could have woken me and said you wanted to read and I would have come with you."

"I just wanted some me time. I am so sorry."

Grabbing me roughly, he smashes his lips into mine passionately, I melt into him and moan. Breaking the kiss, leaving me breathless, he says, "Next time talk to me."

"What do you mean next time?"

"You are so accident-prone Annie, be glad Ry hasn't wrapped you in bubble wrap yet."

Snickering, I reply.

"You are joking, right?"

"Don't be too sure, Annie. I thought he was gonna have a heart attack when he saw that lump on your head."

We walk hand in hand through the house and out into the garden. Max leads me to a beautiful wildflower meadow and I notice a blanket and picnic laid out in the middle.

"When did you have time to do this?"

"I had asked the kitchen to organise this earlier for lunchtime, but someone disappeared. I hope everything is still cool."

"Thank you."

We sit down and Max opens the basket to reveal an array of fruit, sandwiches and pastries. Beside the basket is an ice bucket with a bottle of wine chilling inside. I pour the crisp wine into glasses while Max puts food on our plates.

I take my plate from Max and bite into a strawberry. It tastes like British summer. It is still cool from the icepacks and I end up with juice running down my chin. Reaching over, Max gently licks the juice from my face causing giggles to squeak out of me. We eat our picnic, talking and giggling like any normal relationship, forgetting the recent horrors for a little while. The basket empty, we lay on the blanket feeling a little buzzed from the wine and start to cloud watch.

"Max? Is there any news on Giovanni?"

"Only that he has gone underground, so he is difficult to track."

"Oh, is it safe to have our wedding next week?"

"Annie, with the amount of security we are having, he would be stupid to turn up."

I sigh with relief.

"Good, because Debra has asked me to go for the last fitting for my dress tomorrow, I hope you and Ryan have your suits sorted."

"Yes, Annie, we have, we are going to have a perfect day, your dream wedding."

I smile widely.

"You men really are a woman's wet dream."

Max rolls so he is straddling me.

"I hope we are not just a dream for you as Ry and I have dibs on all your pleasure."

He rolls his hips showing me how much he enjoys my mention of wet dreams, his raging hard-on touches my clit through my clothes. Leaning down, he kisses and bites my neck, making me yelp.

"Max! I cannot have a hickey for our ceremony, it would ruin the photos."

"He will have to give you a love bite elsewhere then, Annette, so it doesn't spoil them."

Max and I look up to see a very amused Ryan, who is wearing his shirt and suit trousers from work, minus his tie.

"That. I should thank you for that brilliant idea, Ry."

Max lowers his body and removes my shorts and panties, chucking them to one side and places his lips on my inner thigh and begins to suck on my skin, making his mark. Ryan comes and kneels at my head and kisses me softly but firmly. We spend the remaining light hours kissing and making love till the moon is shining, the stars twinkling and we are completely sated.

The following morning, I am accompanied to the bridal shop by Martin and one of his colleagues. This was after a long discussion with Ryan in the early hours of this morning, but I make them stand outside the door, so they can't give any clues to the men. I stand on a little round stage as the seamstress goes around, making sure everything fits perfectly.

"Miss Delaney, your dress is perfect, you are going to look a million bucks on your big day."

"Thank you so much."

"Debra will deliver it and your accessories on the morning of your wedding and help you into it."

As I go to thank the seamstress again, Martin barges in from outdoors.

"Miss Delaney, time to go, we spotted Giovanni's right-hand man at the corner of the street."

"Oh, shit, can't they just fuck off now?"

Martin stands outside the changing room as Debra and the seamstress rush to get me back into my regular clothes.

"I am so sorry ladies, I didn't mean to put you in danger," I apologise profusely.

"We will be fine, get yourself to safety."

Martin hurries me out of the shop, just as we get to the car, shots are fired towards us, they ricochet off the bulletproof glass of the windscreen and Martin drives like a bat out of hell to get us away.

"Martin, what about your man?"

"He will be fine. He is in pursuit, he was in the army before he joined us so he is very capable."

I hang onto my seat for dear life as Martin speeds through the outskirts of town towards home.

Ring-Ring

Martin answers on the in-car hands-free.

"Martin, what's happening? Why have I just received a call from Eddie that he is in pursuit and has lost sight of the man?"

"Giovanni's right-hand man was spotted at the corner of the street from the dress shop."

"For fuck's sake, your men are meant to be keeping an eye on those pricks. Is Annette okay?"

"Ryan, I am fine, I am nearly home, and it isn't Martin's fault."

"Fine. Martin, get her here in one piece."

The call is disconnected.

As we hit the gravel drive, Martin nearly spins the car.

"Martin, Ryan said one piece, please."

Martin curses under his breath and pulls up outside the house.

"Go indoors and find your men, ASAP."

Sprinting up the steps, I crash through the door and I am grabbed by two strong arms. My screams are cut short by a hand over my mouth.

"Annie, Annie! It's me, calm down you are safe."

He lets me go and I spin and hug him tightly.

"What is going on, Max?"

"Ryan is briefing the security team, Martin has gone to collect Eddie, and you and I are going to the panic room till this all blows over."

"Max, you have a panic room? Do you have any idea how crazy that sounds? It's like a Hollywood film."

"Of course, you would find humour in a dire situation. Yes, we have a panic room."

He leads me to the library, checking as we go for threats. In the library, he rushes to the far corner and slides a large painting to one side and a keypad is revealed, he types in a code and a huge clank sounds. The door that opens must be a foot thick. Inside is a dark staircase. We go down using Max's phone as a torch, the door shuts automatically behind us.

Max flicks a switch and the lights flick on to reveal a bed, a sofa and a TV. There is a small kitchenette to one side and another door next to it.

"What's behind that door?"

"There is a corridor with three rooms, a bathroom, a pantry with enough food for years, a bathroom with a shower and a room that has computers linked up to the CCTV around the house."

"Okay, what happens now?"

"We wait for a signal from Ryan that the threat has gone."

I look at him sadly.

"I'm scared. I can't lose Ryan."

"We will not lose him, Annie, he is the best shot I know."

I walk away and enter the room with the computers and turn them on. Lots of men swarm the screens, some in masks and shooting at our security. I sit and sob at the scene unfolding, searching for a sign my love is safe. Then I see a man I recognise, but sadly it isn't the one I'm looking for, instead, it is the bastard that has been plaguing us for months. I see Ryan enter the room and I scream.

"Get out, Ryan! He's there waiting for you!"

Chapter Twenty

Bang-Bang

I cover my eyes at the gunshots and scream at the top of my lungs, Max comes running into the room.

"Annie, what is the matter?"

"Giovanni was in a room and there were two gunshots."

"Fuck, who got shot, Annie? Who was it?"

"I don't know, I looked away."

"Okay, I am going to rewind the footage and see who it is, you can stay if you want, it is your choice, but whoever it is, it will not be pretty."

"I will stay, I have to know."

Max rewinds the tape and presses play, the image shows when Ryan steps into the frame and Giovanni raises his Glock and Ryan spins at the hammer click and draws his own weapon. Ryan shoots Giovanni and hits his thigh making him go down onto his knees, the freak raises his arm and lets off a shot, hitting my Ryan.

"Fuck, Ryan. Annie, it was only his shoulder. He will be fine."

Ryan falls to the floor as Giovanni's men drag the man away and out of the house. Our own men grab Ryan and drag him outside to a car and presumably to the hospital. In another part of the panic room, there is an alarm blaring, Max races to the walkie-talkie which is blaring on the table.

"Hello, it's Max here, over."

"Max, it's Martin here, Ryan is in hospital, safe. We managed to kill 15 of Giovanni's men, but the bastard escaped yet again, this is getting very old now. Is Miss Annette well?"

"No, she isn't, she was watching the screens. I think she is in shock, send our clean-up crew round so she doesn't have to see how they redecorated the house, let me know when it's done so we can see our man."

"Yes, sir, will do."

"Annie, it will be over soon."

I sit on the floor shaking and crying, rocking back and forth. Max sits beside me and pulls me into his lap, shushing me.

"We will get to the hospital soon and see Ry, he will be all patched up and cursing he didn't get the cunt in the head."

I sob silently into his shoulder, my body feels like it's being ripped apart.

I will kill that motherfucker myself.

"Max, what is the code for the door?"

"Annie, what are you planning? Why do you want to leave?"

"LET ME OUT MAX, NOW!"

"Annie, no I can't, I am not risking you."

"Tell me the code or so help me God."

Max holds me tighter and shushes me as I rage like a caged animal.

The alarm starts up again and Max answers.

"Martin, you better have some good news. I can't keep her down here much longer."

"We haven't finished the clean-up but we can take her out of the house from a way that she isn't exposed to anything unsavoury."

"I don't give a flying fuck about unsavoury, let me out so I can see Ryan."

"Yes, Ma'am, we will be at the door in two minutes."

Max leads me to the door and opens the door for the security, and about ten men, including Max, lead me out of the house to an awaiting car. We are driven to the hospital, we break every speed limit on the way. Not waiting for the car to make a complete stop, I sprint out the car into the A&E reception.

"Excuse me, my fiancée has been brought in with a GSW. His name is Ryan Matthews."

"Okay, Ma'am. I will look at our system, please try to remain calm."

"Remain calm? My best friend and one of loves of my life got shot today."

"Yes, Madam, I understand that it is traumatic but breathe. Now, he is down the corridor, first door on the left, but he will be going to surgery soon to get the bullet out. You can wait in his room."

I run to his room only to find it empty, he must be in surgery. Max appears moments later.

"Are you okay? Where is Ryan? Is he in surgery?"

"No, surgery, yes."

He holds me to him while we wait for news.

"I guess I have to return my dress." I try and lighten the mood unsuccessfully.

"No of course not, Ryan will just be wearing a sling in the wedding pictures."

"For fuck's sake, he had to ruin my photos, eh?"

"Our photos will be lovely, and I think he will be in too much pain after surgery for you to berate him for that."

A nurse comes into the room to update us.

"Mr Matthews is nearly finished in surgery, it was successful, when he was being wheeled into theatre he said to me to apologise to you about some pictures. I hope that makes sense to you."

Max and I giggle at each other and thank the nurse. A few moments later, Ryan is wheeled in, he looks deathly pale and there is a huge bandage on his shoulder.

"Oh, Ryan."

I lean down and kiss his forehead. He is hooked up to all sorts of machines.

"Max, he doesn't look okay."

"Well, that's a bit fucking rude, I thought the vows say in sickness and in health, we aren't even married and you are trying to get out of it…"

I look at the bed and Ryan has his eyes open and is trying to sit up.

"Ryan, you are awake!"

I hug him tightly, causing a pained groan.

"Fuck, I am so sorry, how are you feeling?"

"Bloody sore and even more pissed off, I didn't have my guard up as much as I should have, and I just thought that Giovanni's goons are stupid."

Max gazes over at his best friend with tears in his eyes.

"Ry, you fucking idiot, but I am glad that you are alive, you big lug. Annie saw you go down first, she was scared, we both were."

Ryan looks at me sadly.

"I am so sorry you saw that."

"I am fine, better now I know that you are okay."

After a few hours of rest, Ryan is allowed home. We spend the rest of the day sitting and watching movies. The guys are not impressed with my lovey-dovey choices. We fall asleep, my head on Ryan's lap and my feet over Max's. The following morning, I help Ryan dress and put on his sling, he grumbles and complains but is happier when I give him his pain relief.

"You are turning into a druggie, Mr Matthews." I tease.

"Yeah, I am, but they feel so good," he jokes back.

He kisses my cheek, smiling down at me.

"Three days till you become my wife, I cannot wait."

"Neither can I, I can't wait to see you and Max in your suits."

Ryan and I make our way out to the garden for breakfast, Max left hours ago to go make sure everything is done correctly before the wedding and our honeymoon.

For breakfast today, we are having a fruit platter, with all colours, shapes and sizes, there is some I recognise and some I don't.

"Ryan, I would like to add a fountain to the gardens. I have always thought they are beautiful."

"After the wedding and honeymoon, we will go and have a fountain made to your specifications, and if you would like, we can add some lavender to the walled garden and you can make it your own."

"Thank you, Ryan, I would love that."

We finish our breakfast and Ryan goes into his office to make sure all the loose ends are sorted. I, on the other hand, go and sunbathe so I am lightly tanned for my wedding.

Splash-Splash

Bolting upright with a shout, "What the fuck, Max?"

He stands over me holding a huge bucket, chuckling to himself.

"You looked like you were burning and needed to cool off. I was only trying to help the damsel in distress."

"I am soaked, Maximus. You are uncouth and mean to me."

I snatch the bucket off him and storm inside the house looking for ice and water, I fill it as much as I can carry and go in search for Max to enact my revenge. I find him in the gym doing bicep curls, looking rather sexy and attractive. It makes me do a double-take. The bucket slips from my hand and hits the floor, soaking me even more.

"Well, that worked well for you, didn't it?"

He places his weight back onto the stand and walks towards me holding a gym towel, he passes it to me grinning like an idiot, and I quickly dry myself, cursing my future husband.

I go and look for Jemma to ask about a mop to clean up the mess I made. "Jemma! There you are, I am sorry to be a pain, may you point me in the direction of a mop, I made a spillage of water trying to soak Max as he interrupted my sunbathing."

"Miss Delaney, I will clean it for you. I have done my chores for today, so I am not busy, but next time let me know when you want to play a joke on Mr Romano and I will set it up for you so you don't make a mess." She chuckles.

"Thank you, Jemma, I will."

"Any time, Madam."

"Please call me Annie."

"Of course, Annie."

We go our separate ways and I head to my room to change. Scrolling through the wardrobe, I select a black skin-tight dress that hugs my curves and some black boots, I put my hair up in a ponytail and release a few tendrils of hair to frame my face, I put on some black eyeliner and some scarlet red lipstick to match my hair.

Knock-Knock

"Annette, you look nice, you going somewhere?"

"Yes, I am. It's my bachelorette party tonight. Luke and I are going to a bar with Katy and having a few drinks."

"I am not going to argue with you as you need your fun, just take some men with you, but promise me you will be safe."

"I promise, Ryan. You and Max need a bachelor night."

"Okay, sweetheart, we will. Martin will drive you in the bulletproof SUV to settle my nerves."

"Yes, sir. How is your arm?" I say, looking at his sling.

"Still aches, but I am happy I got all my work done today. Now, my love, let's get a drink inside you so you can start your night off the right way."

We go to the liquor cabinet in Ryan's office and he pours me a large rum and hands it to me, I gulp it down in one swig, enjoying the warming sensation as it goes down.

"I love you, Annette, you are my little firecracker. Now, off you go and have a good evening."

"Thank you, love you, I will."

I head off and arrive at the bar and find Luke in the garden having a smoke.

"Hey, Tubs! I am here."

"Hello, you soon-to-be-ball-and-chain."

I shove him and chuckle.

"Rude prick, you are lucky you are my best friend, or I would punch your head in."

He hands me a large drink and a cigarette, slapping L-plates onto my ass.

"You are lucky that Ryan and Max aren't here. You would end up on your arse."

He chuckles, knowing I wouldn't let them lay a finger on him.

I sip my drink and look out for Katy.

"Luke, have you seen Katy?"

"She just texted, she is just around the corner."

Katy arrives holding a giant inflatable penis.

"What the fuck have you got that for?" I snicker.

She bonks my head with the balls and grins at me.

"Well, you're marrying two men. Just thought you'd like another to add to your collection, you whore," she says good-naturedly.

The three of us go and grab more drinks from the bar and go sit outside and enjoy the chilled air of the evening.

"So, Annie? Who has the bigger dick out of the two guys?" Katy chortles.

"Both men are above average, but Max is thicker."

"Ew! Yucky, Annie. I do not need to know that, you will have to find someone else to walk you down the aisle if you keep talking like that," Luke says.

"You wouldn't do that to me, you love me way too much to ruin my big day, don't you?"

"You are one lucky bitch, you know I could never let you down."

He hugs me tightly.

We are all very drunk by the end of the night. Martin drives my intoxicated arse home.

"Good night, Madam?"

"Yes, thank you, Martin. Jesus, I drank way too much."

He chuckles and pulls up outside the house and my men are waiting at the door.

"Max, Ryan, are you okay?"

I stumble up the steps to them. I hiccup and giggle to myself.

"Martin rang us when you stumbled out of the bar to pre-warn us."

I trip up the top step and nearly hit the deck but Max's strong arms catch me.

"Bloody hell, Annie, how much did you drink?"

"Too much, been on the rum."

"Annette, let's get you to bed."

"Oh, yeah, you two can take me to bed anytime."

"No, Annette, we are taking you to bed to sleep, nice try."

"No fair! I want some fun."

"Tomorrow, Annie, we promise."

They carry me up to my bed and help me undress, then tuck me into bed after drinking some water, they both kiss me goodnight, chuckling at my overindulgence and leave me to sleep.

Jemma wakes me the following morning with a steaming pile of waffles with syrup and a large glass of gorgeous apple juice.

"Thank you, Jemma. Where are the guys?"

"They have gone to the cabin, they have organised a pamper day for you to get ready for tomorrow and they are using the cabin to prepare themselves."

"But Max promised me fun today."

I pout like a petulant child.

"Max said you would mention that and he told me to tell you that your wedding night will make up for that."

Jemma looks mildly uncomfortable in discussing my sex life.

"Okay, so what have they planned?"

"You have a massage in half an hour followed by a manicure and pedicure, then this afternoon you have a hair appointment."

"Thank you, Jemma, I will just eat this then jump into the shower."

"Very well, Ma'am."

She leaves me to it and I bite into the sweet steaming pile of heaven.

The masseuse has hands that were made by the angels, I swear. I relax so much, the poor man has to wake me and wipe my drool off his massage bed. I mumble my apologies and head off for my mani-pedi. I go for a simple French polish on both, elegant and understated. I am enjoying the thoughtfulness of my soon to-be-husbands. I have a huge buffet lunch made for me by the kitchen. I go and thank the chef profusely.

"You are most welcome. Thank you for making the boys so happy, it is a much nicer household since you joined it."

"Thank you so much, that means a lot to me."

"Now, go and enjoy your day, I have much to prepare for the many guests arriving tomorrow."

I wave my goodbyes and meet Martin in the foyer and he drives me to my hair appointment.

My hair is cut and dyed a deep red and put into curlers ready for tomorrow, I thank and pay the lovely lady even when she tries to refuse. She says she will be at mine early in the morning to style my hair for the wedding.

Chapter Twenty-One

It is my wedding day!

Drinking a mimosa while my hair is styled in an up-do with tendrils framing my face, Debra is running around like she has a rocket up her arse, talking to people on her hands-free earpiece.

"Every table has to have a flower arrangement and a balloon centrepiece."

"Debra, can you ask them to put the wedding favours to the left of the cutlery?"

"Yes, of course."

Frankie is taking lots of pictures of the morning.

"Frankie, make sure you get photos of her shoes and dress before they are put on."

"Are you ze photographer, Madam Debra? I know what pictures to take," Frankie argues but goes to do as he is told.

When my hair is done, I get into my wedding night lingerie and Frankie takes a few boudoir photos to surprise my men. At long last, it is time to step into my beautiful gown, Debra holds my hand to help me to get into it.

Knock-Knock

"Annie, can I come in? It's Luke"

"Yeah, come in. I am in my dress now."

The door opens to a very dapper-looking Luke in his light grey suit. He has a pale lavender pocket square, ties and a white rose buttonhole.

"Bloody hell, Annie! You have scrubbed up well."

"Speak for yourself, Tubs. Looking handsome."

He hugs me very carefully, making sure he doesn't crinkle my dress.

"And I thought I would end up selling ya to get you off my hands."

I swipe at him, nearly toppling on my heels.

"Steady, Annie, can't have you arrive at your wedding with a broken nose because of your clumsiness."

I shake my head and laugh, "Debra, can you please attach my knife to my thigh under my dress, please? Cannot take any risks today."

She tuts at me, rolling her eyes, but clambers under my dress and does as she is told.

Luke and I exit the house. Jemma holds the back of my dress to keep it off the floor as we descend the steps. Waiting at the bottom is a Cinderella-style carriage pulled by four grey horses with lavender plumes attached to their bridles. I gasp at the beauty of it and Jemma and Luke pour me into it. I push my skirts down so Luke can get into the carriage as well. Then we are off to my big day.

"Not changing your mind, Annie? I can hide you if you are."

"Nope, not even a little bit."

"Good, they better treat you right or they will have me to answer to, you deserve the best."

I smile and tears begin to sting my eyes.

"Don't you dare cry, I don't know how to apply make-up, you would end up looking like Black Veil Brides (A rock group we both like) in all your wedding photos."

I blink away the tears and smile at him.

"You are the best, you know that, right?"

"Of course, I do."

We pull up just around the corner from the venue and my beautiful Midnight is there waiting for me in all her finery in a white bridle and saddle with beautiful flowers braided into her mane and tail. Luke takes the reins and leads me towards the most important day in my life. When we get to the gravel drive of the barn, Train's '*Marry me*' starts to play.

At the door of the barn, Luke helps me dismount as carefully as he can and hands me my bouquet. As we enter, the music changes to *'How long will I love you'* by Ellie Goulding. Luke takes my arm and slowly leads me down the aisle. Around the edge of the barn are men dressed in suits with earpieces in, they must be the security that Ryan ordered. I look to the end of the aisle and see my two men looking so handsome. Max is in a grey suit like Luke's, but his usually unruly hair is tied back in a man bun. Ryan is in a black suit, with a matching pocket square to Luke. Being the only colour of his outfit, it makes his eyes stand out, and even his sling is black to hide it in photos. Between them is the vicar that agreed to do the unusual service for us. There must be two hundred guests sitting in the barn.

So much for small and intimate.

Both men smile at me as I reach the end, I have tears in my eyes again as I gaze at my men, amazed that they would want someone like me.

"We are gathered here today in this extraordinary ceremony to join Annette Marie Delaney to both Ryan James Matthew and Maximus Alfonso Romano to be wedded partners."

I think I zone out staring at my men until the priest says, "Do you take these men as your husbands?"

I mumble out, "I do, yes."

"You may kiss your bride."

Ryan steps up first and kisses me deeply and passionately, causing whoops from the guests.

"Show off," Max mutters softly.

Max kisses me deeply, but all too quickly.

"The rest is for tonight," He whispers into my ear.

There are cheers and shouts as we all walk down the aisle to the garden outside, which is our venue for the after-party.

Ryan grabs my left hand and says, "Do you like your wedding band?"

I didn't notice it being put on.

I look at my hand and notice an intricate silver ring that complements my engagement ring.

"It is beautiful, thank you."

The men peel off and greet the guests.

"Landed on your feet here, eh girly?" My mother slurs from behind me.

"Do not ruin this day with your bloody alcoholism, mother."

"Do not disrespect me, child."

I storm away from her as the DJ speaks over the microphone.

"Ladies and gentlemen, it is time for the first dance with Annette and Ryan."

129

'In case You Don't live forever' by Ben Platt comes on over the speakers and Ryan holds out his hand for me to take. We walk to the makeshift dance floor and he spins me slowly and sings to me softly repeating the words.

"I'm everything I am, because of you."

I smile broadly at him and whisper, "I love you so much."

As the song ends, he dips me low and kisses me.

The DJ says, "Beautiful. Now, Annette and Max."

There is scattered applause as Max takes my arm. John Legend's *'All of Me'* plays as Max twirls me around. He gazes at me like I am the most precious thing in all the world. The song ends and Max kisses my temple.

"Thank you for that dance, wife."

"You are most welcome, husband."

"And by the way, the song is true, I don't know what I would do without your smart mouth."

I chuckle and whisper, "Not much I hope."

I wander off and look in awe at the beautiful array of cakes and sweets. Debra has outdone herself with all the decorations. There are beautiful fairy lights twinkling amongst the flower arrangements in the middle of the tables. The whole place feels like it was taken out of a magical storybook. The DJ announces food is ready so we all take our seats. The starter is a prawn cocktail, which tastes like the ocean. It is mouth-watering.

"Ryan? Max? Are you enjoying yourselves?" I look to each of the men on either side of me.

"Yes," they say in perfect harmony with their mouths stuffed. I chuckle and take a long swig from my champagne, the crisp bubbles tickle my taste buds. Between the starter and main, we have a photo session with Frankie and the guests.

"Now, all you lovely people say cheese!"

We all smile brightly.

Flash-Flash

We end up taking beautiful photos for about half an hour before the DJ pipes up.

"Please, all head back to your seats, your main course is served."

The main is tender ham and Chantenay carrots and steamed vegetables, cooked to perfection.

"Time to cut the cake, which has been made by the bride's friend, Katy."

My men and I walk over to the cake and I could not be prouder of Katy. The three-tiered cake is iced with pure white fondant and dainty leaves and sugar flowers. On the top is three models of Ryan, Max and myself, all professionally made by my talented friend. I stand by the cake with my husbands on either side of me. They hold my hand and we cut the first slice together while Frankie takes lots of photos. There is huge applause and Max feeds me as elegantly as his beefy hands can manage. I eat it gratefully as the zesty lemon sponge hits my tongue. The waiters then slice and hand out the cake to all the guests and the security. The DJ starts his set for the night and we all get up and dance.

After a few drinks, I am starting to feel a little buzzed, I have changed into the 1950s style dress I just had to buy, too, to be able to move more freely. My men dance with other guests while I sit for a moment as my heels are beginning to make my feet ache. Ryan brings his mother over to me.

"Mum, this is my wife, Annette."

"So, you are the woman that has swept my boys off their feet. I must say your wedding has been stunning, you have good taste."

"Thank you, Mrs Matthews, I am glad you could make it."

"Annette, you are part of the family now. Please call me mum or Lauren."

"You are not her mother, I am."

My mother dearest screeches from behind my new mother-in-law, making me cringe.

"Mum, go home, you are not ruining my night."

Martin steers my mother to a taxi to avoid a scene, giving me a smile as he does and sends her on her way.

"I'm sorry, Lauren, my mother likes a tipple and can be obnoxious with it."

"That is perfectly alright, my dear. Now you enjoy your night." She embraces me tightly, then Ryan and his mother go back to the dance floor and have a few dances.

I nip to the ladies' room to relieve myself and look into the mirror, I am flushed and look the happiest I have ever had. Exiting the bathroom, I bump into a gentleman wearing a suit.

"Sorry, I am a little tipsy."

"Do not worry, you are allowed to be on your big day."

His accent sounds mildly Italian, but my foggy brain pays it no mind and I head back to the party.

Chapter Twenty-Two

I greet my men on the dance floor and begin to dance with Max, my skirts flowing out like a tutu.

"Annie, when you spin, I can see you're carrying your knife, are you okay?"

"Can never be too careful at the moment."

"That is a fair statement, now let me slow dance you again, I want to hold you."

We slow dance even though a quick-paced song is playing. I gaze up at my man, drinking in his handsome features.

"How did I get so lucky marrying two amazing men?"

"Because you are so unique, it takes two to handle you."

I playfully shove him away and giggle.

"You are so bloody rude, Mr Romano."

"Only to you, Mrs Romano-Matthews."

We laugh and dance together, enjoying the moment of pure contentment. Drinks are handed to us as Luke decides he is going to make a toast.

Oh dear, what is the cheeky prick going to say?

"Hello to all the guests who have come to this exceptional day, the day my best friend marries her two loves. I have known Annie for many years, and I have seen her ups and downs. I know a funny story or two as well."

"Don't you dare!" I shout up to him.

"My favourite one to tell is the time she first got very drunk. We were down the woods with friends and had to walk home. I decided to take a shortcut over a gate. Annette got stuck by the arse of her trousers on a split part of the wood and could not get herself free. I couldn't help her for laughing, but eventually she got herself free, but at the expense of the seat of the trousers, so she had to walk home with a massive hole in them."

The crowd chuckles and I go bright red.

"Now, I am so happy for Annie, but glad I didn't have to pay someone to take her off my hands. Max. Ryan. You have your work cut out with that one, I tell ya. She's a strong-headed little shit when she wants to be."

"We know, she's as stubborn as an ox," Max shouts his response. The crowd murmurs their agreements.

"Now, a toast to wedding bliss for our favourite throuple."

The sound of clinking glasses surrounds us.

I hear a gurgling, strangling sound from my left and turn to see one of the guards flop to the floor with his throat slit, standing in his place is none other than Giovanni and his right-hand man, the man I had bumped into earlier outside the toilet. Guests start shrieking as they notice the limp body on the floor, surrounded by a pool of fresh blood. A panic starts to ensue. My men stand next to me as a protective barrier, I remove my knife from its holster, the twinkly lights glint off my sharp deadly weapon.

I'm glad I changed dresses.

It seems to rain our men down on the two wedding crashers. There are shouts and screams as Giovanni tries to fight off the men. I hear bones being broken and one of our security runs back to us with his arm bent the wrong way, making my stomach flip. I walk towards the bundle of men, knife in hand, Max pulls me gently towards him by my shoulder and shakes his head. Seconds later, the two men are restrained and on their knees, both their noses are broken and blood dripping onto their clothes. Our security guards panting hard.

"*Mi Amore*, you look positively ravishing."

Giovanni practically spits at me.

That comment earns him a punch in the teeth from Max. Another man comes running towards us screaming in Italian, with a gun raised. He fires five shots one after the other, hitting a few of the security men.

I'm sick of this shit.

Ignoring the shouts from Ryan and Max, I barge past them towards the gunman and stab him in the ear, taking him by surprise as he was focused on helping Giovanni, he lets out a guttural scream and flops to the floor. Giovanni starts to scream and shout, cursing me. Martin looks at my men, shrugging his shoulders.

Ryan whispers, "Well done for putting him out of action, but you might not be so lucky next time taking a knife to a gunfight, I will end up punishing you for your absolute disregard for your safety."

"What shall we do with them, boss?"

Ryan looks over to Martin and nods firmly.

"Clear the remaining guests here and take the Italians to the ruins down the path and keep him there. We shall join you in a moment."

"Yes, sir."

"I am coming with you, I am going to get my revenge on this hateful bastard." My voice is laced with venom.

I am practically shaking with rage at the man who ruined my party and made my life hell the past few months. The man who sexually assaulted me and darkened my dreams.

My husbands decide against fighting and nod, seeing just how angry I am. Once the guests have cleared, we walk down the path towards the sounds of pained screams, I smile sadistically. I see Giovanni's man on the floor curled into a ball, with Martin kicking in his chest.

"Enough, Martin."

Martin backs away and leaves the man coughing blood on the floor. Storming up to the man who has haunted my nightmares for months and take out my blade in one fluid motion and spin it over my fingers in a practised gesture, making the Italian coward gulp.

"Now, Giovanni, what do you say we play a little game?"

I laugh maniacally at the man, my body on adrenaline over drive.

Before I get a response, I stab him as hard as I can manage in his meaty thigh muscle, feeling my knife hit his bone and twist and pull it out, causing blood to pour out of the gaping wound. Enjoying his enraged screams at me, next I remove his right ear with one swift slice. The blood splatters onto my dress but I no longer care, I am torturing my tormentor and I am in my element, this is healing my pain. Max and Ryan are standing behind me, waiting for my rage to simmer down to take over.

"You fucking, cunning bitch, I will kill you for this."

The now faeces smelling snake curses at me, making me smile broadly.

"It's true, men do shit themselves when they are going to die."

135

I chuckle to myself.

"Have you pissed yourself, too? Big strong mafia man now degraded to a whimpering wreck at the hands of a woman, what a shame."

Max hands me a pair of pliers, enjoying my strength to face this man.

"These are effective at removing extremities."

I use it to snap off all of Giovanni's fingers one by one. Then I take my knife and remove his other ear. The bloodied man has stopped his string of curses now as he is almost dead from blood loss, I take some vodka and pour it into his wounds causing him to scream again. My body slumps as the adrenaline leaves my body in a rush. Ryan comes up behind me and holds me.

"My love, he is nearly done. Is there anything else you wish to do? Have you got the revenge you so desired?"

I nod and stab the prick in his prick for good measure, well, where I think it would be, can't be sure it's big enough to stab.

"Done now, thank you."

Ryan turns me away, hiding my face into his chest as Martin's hands Max a gun, he approaches the man, gun in hand, cocking it as he gets close.

Bang

The sound makes me flinch as it brings back flashbacks of Ryan being shot, he squeezes me tightly to him for a moment and I look at him concerned.

"Ry, my love, is your shoulder okay?"

"Yes, darling it is, are you okay? You seemed out of it while beating the shit out of Giovanni."

"I am deliriously happy that it is all over, I am glad I got to hurt him like he did me, I can finally be at peace."

"Okay, sweetheart, let's head home and clean up. Then we can go on our honeymoon, we can move on with our life now."

"What about his right-hand man?" I ask, concerned one is still breathing.

"Martin can deal with him and then both bodies unless you have something to show that one too?"

"No, Ryan, I want to start our life and put all this hatred and horror behind us."

We walk off into the night, Max trailing behind. The sound of flesh being sawn echo's around us.

Back at home, my new husbands help me remove my dress as I am now shaking like a leaf.

"Annie, you did so well, you were lethal and beautiful, I swear I had a hard-on watching you work."

"Maxy, you really are a perverted arse."

"Annette, you did look like a dancer with your knife, we were so proud of you, my love. The training has paid off."

They both smile widely down at me, take me to the bath and lower me into the warm bubbles, the scent of lavender relaxes me, my eyes close and my men kiss my forehead.

"Annie, do you want us to help you wash? You look exhausted."

"Please, my muscles have stopped working."

"Annette, that is because you have exerted yourself, it is not easy to push a blade into someone's brain. Now, I will wash your hair while Max washes your body as we have to leave to catch our flight in an hour and you can sleep on the plane."

I swear I could orgasm at my men massaging my aching body as they wash me, it is heaven, what a way to end a long day.

I dress into some comfy clothes; leggings and a black vest top, my hair is still up in the up-do from the wedding, but I have removed my veil. Jemma has kindly packed my suitcase, but I am a little suspicious of the grin that is on her face.

What the hell has she packed?

I put some sandals on my feet and I am ready to go, Martin comes and grabs my bag.

"Are you okay Martin, is everything sorted?"

"Yes, Madam. Are you well after the experience?"

"Yes, I am relieved it is over, Martin. I am going on my honeymoon to new countries and I'm excited to be having something normal in my life."

"That is good, I know your husbands have plenty of surprises for you along the way."

"Tell me, tell me, tell me! Please."

"Annette, stop hassling poor Martin. The poor man is probably exhausted after tonight's trials."

"It is fine, sir, she was asking about the surprises you and Mr Romano have planned, but I am like Fort Knox, nothing is coming out of my mouth."

"We know, Martin, it is just fun winding her up." Max chuckles.

"You lot are bloody mean to me."

That only precedes in making them laugh like a bunch of hyenas. We clamber into the large SUV that Ryan is so proud of and head off to the airport and our honeymoon.

"A fucking private jet? You two never mentioned to me that you have a private jet, holy fucking hell."

"Max, I think our wife is excited about our mode of transport."

"Ry, I totally agree with you, what is she gonna be like when she sees the bed?"

"There is a bed onboard? This day gets better and better, we can consummate our wedding, then sleep till landing."

"Why, when you put it like that, does it sound like a business transaction, Annie? Sex is supposed to be fun."

Ignoring my spoilt sounding man, I bolt as fast as my legs will carry me up the stairs and into the most luxurious plane I have ever seen. The chairs are more like recliner armchairs and there is so much room, the air hostess is busy making drinks for us, the pilot shakes my hand and introduces himself, but I don't hear him as I am too busy looking around in awe. We take our seats, ready for take-off and I am guzzling down the drink the beautiful air hostess handed me a few moments before.

"Annie slow down or you won't get your wish of joining the mile-high club, you will just be in an alcohol-induced sleep till we get to Rome."

I ignore him again and continue to slug it back. The fasten seatbelt sign flashes up and I buckle in, ready for this journey.

"Annie, why are you ignoring us?"

"Because, Maxy, you were horrible about us making love."

"I'm sorry, Annie, I did not mean to upset you."

I look at him and he genuinely looks sorry.

"It's fine, do not do it again, I am just excited."

He leans over and kisses me.

"Love you, wifey."

"Love you, you big bear."

I look over to Ryan and the air hostess is trying to flirt with my new husband, I just see red. She has undone another button, flashing her ample cleavage into his face. Then she has the audacity to 'accidentally drop something then bend over, the split in her skirt rides up showing her red thong. I stand and storm over to my husband and straddle his lap, kissing him deeply and marking my territory like a cat in heat. Dragging him by the hand, I drag him through to the bedroom.

"You coming, Max? I want both of my husbands in here."

Giving unnecessary emphasis on husbands. The woman looks green with jealousy as I shut the door.

"Now, you two are gonna fuck me so hard the, fucking fish hear us in the ocean."

Both men look confused, but hungry at my statement.

"Your wish is our command, Annie."

Max's voice is now husky with desire. Ryan grabs me and throws me on the bed, following me close behind, kissing and leaving a trail of love bites on my neck, I moan softly at his own territory marking. Max awkwardly removes my shoes while I am under Ryan. They growl like caged wolves, then Ryan gets off me and sits me up. Painfully slowly, they undress me, purposefully caressing my body with their fingertips as they do, making my nerves light up and turning me into a horny wet mess, panting hard and wanting more. Ryan spins me and pushes the front half of my body onto the bed, leaving my feet on the floor and my ass in the air for their viewing pleasure.

Slap-Slap

Ryan's hand connects to my arse cheek, not enough to really hurt but enough to make me jolt forward in surprise.

"I don't think so, this has been coming for a while and you will be cumming soon."

He grabs my hips, pulling me back as Max pushes a cold butt plug into my arse. Ryan slaps my arse again, the tensing of my body is bittersweet as it arouses me more with the object inside my body. Ryan strokes along my slit.

"Mm, are you enjoying this, sweetheart? You are deliciously wet for us."

He pushes his index finger inside me and causes me to moan loudly.

"I think that is a yes, Max, don't you?"

Max grunts a response and climbs onto the bed, positioning himself on my head end, I lick my lips in anticipation.

"Annie, are you hungry for my cock down your throat?"

"Yes," is all I manage to pant out before he begins to fuck my mouth hard enough to make my eyes water. Ryan exchanges his finger for his cock in one fluid motion causing me to scream around Max's cock, spurring him on fucking my throat. Ryan's pace picks up speed and I turn into a mewling mess. Max pulls out of my mouth at the same time Ryan leaves my pussy, I growl at the loss of my men inside me, to which they both chuckle.

"Patience, Annette darling, we are repositioning to make your wish a reality."

Max gets off the bed and helps me to stand while Ryan lays on the bed on his back with his feet touching the floor, Max lowers me onto Ryan's awaiting cock. With dextrous fingers, Max removes the butt plug and throws it across the room and lines his dick up to my other entrance and slides in roughly making me scream loudly, both men then pick up their pace. I moan and scream through my orgasm, making my men speed up to intensify it.

"Max! Ryan! Fuck!" Is the only fairly understandable words I can get out.

Max cums hard into my arse, biting into my shoulder as he does, that sets Ryan's orgasm off filling me to the brim with their seed. We still for a moment panting hard, before dressing and going back to our seats, the jealous bitch is bright red and looking royally pissed off, I get out of my seat and storm up to her.

"Now, these men are both my husbands, when you clean the bedroom, the stain on the sheets is from them fucking me, you have already heard us, so that should be a wake-up call for you, do not ever try and flirt with either of them or I will cut your eyes out and shove them down your throat till you gag on them and I will remove your ample bosom so you cannot flirt with what isn't yours again, do I make myself clear?"

The poor woman stumbles back, her face paling instantly.

"Yes, Ma'am."

"Good, you may call me Mrs Romano-Matthews."

She nods and bolts to the jet's kitchen.

Chapter Twenty-Three

We land several hours later, my men and I joined the mile-high club three times over during it, much to the air hostess's disgust. To be even more of a bitch, I leave my cum filled panties on the bed for her to find.

"Annette, was that really necessary? I wouldn't even go there, I love you."

"I was marking my territory saying you two are off-limits."

They chuckle and lead me to our taxi to the hotel. The hotel is like those in movies; the foyer is all marble and chandeliers, and we have a bellboy who brings our bags up to the suite for us.

The suite is enormous, there is three bedrooms plus a huge bathroom with a pure white claw-footed tub. There is a huge corner sofa in the main room, which is sitting in front of what must be a seventy-inch TV. We even have a huge balcony that looks out to the Coliseum, it looks amazing all lit up in the dusk, even the pale stone pavements around it seem to glow in the light. We all sit outside looking at the city below, sipping on Italian wine, it feels like bliss.

"You two really are amazing, this view is gorgeous."

"Annie, you deserve it, you are our wife and we want to spoil you rotten."

"That is correct, Annette, you are our shining star, we are lucky to call you ours."

"Thank you, I love you both."

Ryan calls room service as I am craving something sweet, and when it arrives, we eat a whole tub of fresh gelato between us, the cool sweet dessert is like sex on a spoon. Max puts the tub in the bin and brings out a huge pink bowed box.

"What is that?"

"Open it and find out, you impatient cow."

I tear off the wrapping and the bow, to find several smaller boxes inside which are all individually wrapped. The first smaller box I open contains a small key ring that has a charm of the Coliseum on it. The second is a beautiful silver necklace, which has a large opal in the shape of a heart, I stare at all the exquisite colours in the precious stone, fascinated at the array of different shades which change in the light.

"That is a radiant gift, it must have cost a fortune, I cannot accept something this big from you, especially when I have already cost you so much."

"Don't be silly, Annie. We want to spoil you after our mess got you into so much trouble."

Tears well in my eyes, this time because of my overwhelming happiness. I reach for the third box, which is the largest, and inside is a dazzling, delicate tiara that is full of sapphires and diamonds. I look at the men, puzzled as to why I need this stunning gift.

"Why did you get me a tiara?"

"Now, Giovanni is dead, Max is now technically the king or boss, and you are our queen."

"Max, how can you be boss? You do not like the mafia."

"Annie, by the laws, I have to reign for a year before I can hand it over."

"You can't. You will end up hurt or worse."

"I won't, Annie, as I will be leading remotely from the UK, and now Giovanni and his lackey are dead, the rest have always been loyal to me and any that aren't will be weeded out by our men and either exiled or terminated."

I am not convinced.

"Are you sure, Max?"

"Yes, I am, now open the last box."

I open the last box a bit more carefully than I did the last few and nestled inside is a gold signet ring, with a symbol on that I do not recognise.

"What is this?"

"Annette, it is a symbol, which in the mafia means you are someone's wife within the organisation and cannot be touched."

"The padre took me but knew who I was to you?"

"You were not Max's wife, that marriage secures your safety, even if legally you are only married to me, the mafia saw the wedding and now you have that ring, you are safe."

"Is that the only reason we got married then?"

"No, of course not Annette, we both love you dearly and are hurt you think that's why we did."

I slip on the ring and twirl it around my right middle finger.

"Thanks you two for your presents, I have one for you."

I go and disappear into the main bedroom and slip on some red-bottomed heels, a push up black bra and some matching underwear and carry out my own two little boxes. When I walk back out to the balcony doors, both men jump out of their seats looking rather aroused, they stand in the way of any creepy paparazzi and I hand each one a box. Max gets into his first and inside is a leather cuff bracelet with A and M engraved onto it in calligraphic writing and a set of dog tags with our wedding date and our names stamped into the silver metal. Next, Ryan opens his gift and he has a silver chain link bracelet with R and A engraved onto it and his own set of dog tags, both men seem amazed at my little gifts.

"Thank you, Annie, these are so thoughtful," Max gushes, putting on his tags. They make a pretty tinkling sound.

"Thank you, Annette, I will treasure these always," Ryan says smiling sweetly.

That night, I sleep soundly after a long lovemaking session with my two astonishing, awe-inspiring husbands.

Ring, Ring
It is six o'clock in the morning. What the fuck?

Max jumps on the bed, narrowly avoiding covering me with a cup of coffee.

"Annie, you are awake? I brought you coffee, we are taking you out to see the city today, come on, we want to leave before the rush of tourists hit the Coliseum."

"Max, its 6 a.m. What the hell?"

He hands me the steaming cup and leaves the room, whistling a chirpy tune to himself. I groan to myself and roll out of bed, downing my coffee in three gulps, scalding my throat as I do so.

Caffeine is good.

I shower, which wakes me up a little, soon after I open my suitcase to find some clothes for the day trip. I finally find some sensible clothes to wear in amongst the erotic outfits that Jemma so kindly packed for me.

I must speak to her about her idea of packing clothes, little cow bag, at least customs didn't want to look in my bag.

I dress in a pale blue t-shirt and denim shorts with white sandals, I throw a large, flowery, cotton scarf over my shoulders as you aren't allowed to have shoulders bare within the city of Rome. I exit the bedroom and meet up with my men. They are in shorts which is unusual attire for them, but they look as drool worthy as always. They grab my hands and we walk towards the Coliseum. There is a little gelato stall just outside and we stop for a cone which I end up spilling down my chin, like the child I am, as I try to eat it quickly before it melts. Once we have eaten it all, we enter the huge, ancient monument. Inside, it is magnificent, the size of the main area is vast and the history is so interesting. I read the exhibits about the gladiators and I am shocked at the amount of detail on each one. There are skulls that have been excavated from the site on display, the amount of animal ones is very depressing and I think about my poor Luna. Max stands next to a huge statue of a muscular man and poses in bodybuilder like positions, making me laugh. I see an empty plinth and climb on top, giving my best vogue poses, which causes my men to laugh and take photos on their phones.

"Max, get up here, you too, Ryan. Give your phone to Martin to take our picture."

They do as they are told and my men balance behind me posing with funny faces and I join in, Martin snaps lots of photos before an angry looking security guard from the exhibits runs over shouting in Italian. Max talks to the man calming in his native tongue and I think apologises for our actions and pulls a wad of euros out of his wallet and hands them to him and the man smiles and nods.

"Well, the kind gentleman isn't going to call the police, but we have been asked to leave."

We all erupt in raucous laughter and leave the area before the man changes his mind.

Sitting outside a tiny little bistro, we eat a delicious seafood tagliatelle, with a fruity, crisp, chilled white wine. We must have explored the entire city today, I have brought lots of little trinkets today for our house, a little bronze statue of a woman for the window in our bedroom, a dream catcher with white shells that have a mother of pearl inside hanging from the tassels which make a pretty

144

tinkling sound in the wind. My favourite purchase of the day is a painting done by a local artist which is lively and full of bright colours. It's very abstract which makes both men screw up their noses. After the pasta, we have a lemon-cello sorbet which cuts through the richness of the pasta, it is so refreshing.

Back at the hotel, my men take me to the hotel pool to cool off, I get them back for the rude comments about my painting by wearing a skimpy bikini, which just covers my nipples and pussy and is a thong in the back, and it is all black with a pink bow between my boobs on the string. I strut by them, bending over at every opportunity. Max gets fed up with my flashing and scoots to the end of his sun lounger, and pushes me sharply causing me to fall into the cool pool, when I resurface, I notice Max has my bikini bottoms in his hand.

"Max, throw them to me, please."

"No, I don't think I will, you wanna flaunt and make us horny in this heat? You need to be taught a lesson."

"MAX!"

He laughs loudly and tosses them to the other side of the pool so I have to do a kinda awkward hop all the way to them, and try to subtly put them on, looking around paranoid another guest will come out to the pool and see me with my pants down.

Enough bloody people have seen me naked.

I swim over to my darling husbands seething at Max, I splash him as hard as I can and swim off to the deep end and float on my back, enjoying the sun on my face and the cool on my body. I lightly swish my arms and legs, feeling like a mermaid. Suddenly, I am dragged under, I kick hard and thrash about my hand connects with something squishy and I manage to surface. Taking a huge gulp of air I come face to face with a very pained looking Max.

"You okay?"

"No, Annie, you punched me in the bollocks."

"Sorry, Max, you startled me."

Max is clutching his crown jewels and looking very red. Ryan falls off his sunbed from laughing so hard.

"You laugh, you really are a prick."

This statement only makes Ryan laugh more, he is on his knees at this point, at the edge of the pool, Max reaches over and pulls him in. Our joint laughter echoes around us, my jaw begins to ache from it.

Back at the room, we wash off the chlorine from our dip, but the temptation to be a little naughty becomes too much for us and we sneak back to the pool at the cover of darkness for a midnight swim, we strip off our clothes and jump in, my gorgeous men swim up to me and kiss me softly, Ryan lifts me onto the side and I lay back my arse hanging off the edge, his fingers explore my pussy in the hushed light. Max climbs out of the pool and lifts my head up to his cock, he cradles my head gently while I lick up and down the shaft. Ryan pushes his fingers into my pussy and lowers his head and sucks on my clit, causing me to buck my hips. He adds a second finger, suckles and laps at my nerve filled bud, my body tenses as the pleasure builds in my lower abdomen, Ryan and Max pick up their pace.

"Annie, cum over Ryan's fingers," Max says in hushed tones.

I cum, my juices coating his fingers, he pulls them out and licks his fingers clean.

"Your juices taste like ambrosia from the Gods, Annette."

Max pulls out of my mouth and swaps place with Ryan, he enters my pussy with one precise stroke within seconds Ryan is fucking my throat hard, making my eyes water. Max holds me tightly as his body slams into mine making my body cum twice before he finds his release, Ryan cums down my throat a few minutes after, we sit there for a few moments panting hard. A large searchlight scans over the pool.

"Sirs, Madam, please leave this pool, it closed hours ago, and please take your clothes with you."

I am so happy we are leaving here to go to the next part of the honeymoon tomorrow.

We run from the pool area giggling like kids, clutching our clothes to our chests, we fall through the room door and sit on the floor in hysterics.

"Mr Matthews, Mr Romano, Mrs Romano-Matthews, glad to see you back," Martin says as he turns the corner to see us, stopping short as he sees our lack of clothing and spins on the spot and bolts away shouting, "Sorry, I will stay in my room tonight."

We slip into our room to dress and then go to find Martin.

"Sorry for giving you such a fright Martin, we were running from an unhappy security guard for the hotel, we had a midnight skinny dip."

Martin chuckles and shakes his head.

"It's fine Ma'am, hope you have had a good evening, now I have a few things to mention about the flight tomorrow, firstly the air hostess who travelled with us here has quit and gone home so I have had to hire a new one, secondly we have to go to Paris before the last location as the pilot needs to grab a few parts for our smaller plane there."

"Okay Martin, Annie has always wanted to see Paris, we can visit the Eiffel tower while the pilot gets the bits he needs, and have you vetted this new woman?"

"Yep, she is as clean as a whistle."

I look at my feet feeling a little guilty at the lady leaving because of me.

"Annette, do not feel guilty, she made you uncomfortable. We should have fired her on the spot. We do not want the staff that make you feel that way."

"I am so sorry. I did not mean to cause you any trouble."

All the men look at me with soft smiles.

"Ma'am I looked into the woman that upset you and she has been fired for similar behaviour before, I don't know why we hired her."

I nod, feeling a little better with Martin's words. Max and Ryan hug me tightly and kiss my temples, we all go our separate ways to get the maximum amount of sleep for the early rise we have tomorrow.

The flight to France takes less time than I expected, but I did fall asleep because of the early start; the boys organised a limo to take us on a quick tour of Paris, we see and go through the Arc de Triompe, pass many markets and drive past the Louvre, before going to the Eiffel tower. We ascend in the famous lift, I take lots of photos of the views, saving them for a scrapbook I plan on making.

"Max, Ryan you can see the spires of Notre Dame up here, it is beautiful, I wonder if we will see Quasimodo swinging around the gargoyles, I cannot believe how breath-taking this is."

"Take a breath Annie, we are here all day."

I grin and try to stop my body from shaking with excitement. At the top, we exit the lift and the boys lead me up a small flight of stairs to a small apartment, in which we find a chef preparing us a brunch.

"Guys, did you organise this for me?"

"Yes, Annette, as we are not here long, we thought that you would like to try French delicacies while we are."

I swear every food in the country ends up on the table in front of me, and I try a small bite of them all. The fresh baguettes melt in my mouth the fluffy dough makes me want to ship the chef home. The frog's legs and snails make my stomach turn, the snails are like salty snot, but apparently, according to the guys they taste like whelks.

I do not want whelks then.

The pastries the chef makes are to die for, sweet and flaky with delicious fillings, with every bite I am offered a different wine to pair it with and by the end of our brunch I feel like a beached whale.

We head back to the airport in the limo, my eyelids get heavier and heavier as we get closer to my lunch from earlier, making me drift into a food coma. I am vaguely aware of being lifted from the car and carried to the plane.

Chapter Twenty-Four

"We are staying in a fucking castle, how the fuck did you two manage this?"

"Annette, this castle belonged to my grandfather who gifted it to me when he died."

"You inherited a sodding castle, my grandmother left me with a silver brooch, fuck me how the other half live, eh?"

Ryan rolls his eyes at me, looking a bit smug. We landed in the highlands of Scotland several hours ago, the drive from the airport was long and bumpy but worth it to see this ostentatious building, I have been pacing on the drive for about half an hour ranting about the fact it is a castle. Martin carries our bags in as an older looking woman in her fifties comes to greet us, her greying hair is tied in a severe bun on the top of her head. She is wearing a black knee-length dress with a crisp white apron.

"Mrs McGraw, this is our wife Annette, how has everything been going since the last time Max and I were here."

"Hello dear, all is well, we were informed of Mr Romano's family troubles so have been extra cautious, but we have had nothing here."

"Good, I am glad to hear it, now what is on for supper?"

"Sir, tonight we have made roast beef and vegetables with gravy."

"Sounds scrumptious, we are going to get settled in."

"Very well, sir."

I watch the conversation between the pair and it is obvious Ryan has a huge amount of respect for the older woman. We go up a grand staircase and into a room with a huge wooden door with metal hinges, inside is a huge, dark wooden four-poster bed which is surrounded by a sheer black curtain which shrouds the bed so from the door you cannot see who is in the bed.

That will be useful if we are going at it like rabbits as we tend to do and Mrs McGraw walks in.

We unpack our cases and put things away, Max and Ryan show me where to put my toiletries and my clothes. They send me for a nice bubble bath to wash off my grunge from travelling. The bathtub is a large deep copper tub with taps in the middle of one side, there are little mesh bags of lavender in a basket beside so I pop one into the warm water and enjoy the subtle scent filling the room, there is a window beside the bath that overlooks the grounds which is attractively kept, everything looks perfectly pruned and the flowers are wonderfully arranged, I step into the steaming water and sigh as the water warms my body.

I wrap myself in a towel, when the water finally goes cold and go to grab some clothes, I am startled by a young woman standing in my room.

"Who the hell are you?"

"Sorry, Ma'am, Mrs McGraw sent me to get you as dinner will be ready soon, your husbands are expecting you."

"I am sorry I shouted, you surprised me, I will dress and be down shortly."

The woman flees and slams the door.

Great first impression, screaming at the poor woman. She only looked nineteen.

I dress in a long floral print maxi dress with some black sandals and leave to go hunting for the dining room, and promptly end up in a kitchen.

"Hey, you, what are you doing in my kitchen?"

"I apologise, sir, I seem to be a bit turned around in this massive place."

"Well, fuck off out of my kitchen."

"Kenneth Andrew McGraw, you are speaking to the wife of Mr Matthews and Mr Romano, watch your tongue." I hear a shriek from behind me, I turn slowly to face who is reprimanding this tree trunk sized man to see Mrs McGraw red-faced and looking furious at her husband.

"Oh bollocks, sorry Ma'am, I didn't know I was talking to the mistress of the house, I don't like interruptions when I cook."

"She is not a mistress. She is the lady of the house and your boss."

The scolded man bows awkwardly in apology.

I hope me and my men are like this in our old age.

"It is okay Mr McGraw, but please do not shout at me again, and both of you please just call me Annie."

The pair smile warmly at me and Mrs McGraw ushers me into the dining room.

"Annie Ma'am, you may call me Maggie, I have known your fine young men since they were babes in arms, I know what has gone on so if you need a friend I am here."

"Thank you, Maggie, I appreciate that, I believe that we will become firm friends."

Maggie clears her throat as we enter what could be called a banquet hall with a long, rectangle table with a huge candelabra in the middle, which has eight lavender scented candles in it. Max and Ryan stand by their respective seats and Ryan pulls out a heavy high-backed chair at the head of the table for me. I smile and take my seat. The food is brought out on silver platters, it all smells heavenly. Maggie dishes up for me like she has been trained in silver service all her life, when we have all started our meal she discreetly exits the room, to let us eat.

After our delicious meal, the boys go for a walk around the vast grounds. I sit with Maggie and sip some scotch whiskey.

"Maggie, how long have you known the guys?"

"Annie, I used to change their nappies when they were wee bairns, I used to care for the children while the adults were at their sinful parties."

"Wow, you have worked for the Matthews family a while then."

"Since I was a fresh-faced eighteen-year-old, I grew up in a nearby village, my mother worked for them till she was in her eighties, so we have been here for a while, yes."

"Well, Maggie I hope you are here for many years to come."

The older woman smiles at me, her face is kind and non-judgmental towards me.

"I will lass, if my stupid husband doesn't get us sacked for his loud mouth."

"He won't, I promise, you have taken care of my men for me and that to me means everything."

"Now Annie, I must get back to work, enjoy yourself here, the whisky is strong though don't drink too much."

She goes inside and I sit, sipping the warming amber liquid slower than I was before heeding the old woman's warning. I pull my phone out of my pocket and message Luke some pictures of our trip so far.

Ding-Ding

Lucky bitch, where was my invite?

It's my honeymoon, you grumpy arse, unless you want to hear me get fucked every night?

Nope, no way, enjoy it without me, but we have to visit that castle soon.

I chuckle and snort to myself.

"What's so funny Annie?"

I pass my phone to my burly husband and he scans the phone, reading the messages, before snickering at Luke's reply.

"Poor Luke is now traumatised from the image of you two fucking me."

"He will get over it, Annie, Ryan has got a few jobs to do around the area so you and I are going up to bed."

"This late, what possible jobs need doing at this time of night?"

"Do not stress yourself. He will be back soon, shall we get you a refill?"

He points to my now empty glass.

"Fine, but he better come back in one piece or I will kill him myself."

"He will don't fret, now come on it's cold out here now."

I stomp inside behind Max and he leads me to a small room which is lined with bottles of alcohol of all shapes and sizes, scanning over the room, he finds the bottle he is looking for quickly pours me a large drink and replaces the bottle. Taking my hand firmly, he leads me up the stairs to our room, we sit on the bed while I finish my drink, he gently strokes my hair and whispers.

"You are the most amazing woman I have met, you have been strong through the whole ordeal. I am in awe of you, my darling Annie."

"Max, you and Ryan have become the most important people in my life, I never thought I could love two people so wholly, thank you so much for being mine."

Kissing my lips softly, he takes my glass and puts it on the bedside table.

"Annie, get into bed, I have to pop out. I will be back soon."

I look up and him and whisper. "Where are you going?"

"Just going to help Ryan with some bits, if you need anything, Mrs McGraw will be downstairs, but try and get some sleep."

I nod solemnly and undress and slip into the soft sheets as Max leaves the room. I toss and turn, unable to settle without my men in the same building. At one in the morning, I head downstairs and grab a glass of water and bump into Mrs McGraw.

"Annie dear, why are you awake?"

"I can't sleep, I miss them."

"I know dear, they will be home soon, now off to bed."

She shoos me upstairs and helps me to bed and turns off the light as she leaves.

I am so worried about what the guys are up to.

I spend the rest of the night laying in bed awake, waiting for the return of my husbands.

Martin tries to soothe my nerves as I wander around the gardens the following morning.

"They have probably got the quad stuck somewhere and are walking home as we speak."

"Martin, I know you are lying to me so please stop and tell me the truth."

"I am, Ma'am, I am telling you the truth."

"Martin, your eyes tell me you're lying, so what are my husbands doing?"

I stomp away, not wanting to hear any more lies. I can't even enjoy the divinely scented flowers that surround me because I am so worried, so I head inside to find Maggie. I head to the kitchen, being mindful to knock first.

"Mr McGraw? May I come in? I am looking for Mrs McGraw."

"Of course, Annie, come in, Maggie is just in the pantry, looking for something to rustle up for breakfast."

I open the door and Mr McGraw motions for me to sit on the chair by the long work surface and continues to chop vegetables.

"Annie, I am making a veg soup tonight, is that okay?"

"Yes, thank you. That will be lovely, I only hope my husbands will be here to enjoy it with me."

"Ah they will lass, as boys they used to disappear for days making my Maggie fretful, but they always returned home when they were ready."

"I hope you are right."

Maggie steps into the kitchen with an armful of eggs and flour and milk, I stand to help her.

"No, no dear, you stay put I am okay, you look pale Annie, did you not go back to sleep?"

"No, I waited for them to return, where are they?"

"Annie, dear, I can honestly say I do not know, I wish I did to give them a good hiding for putting you through this much stress, it isn't good for someone in your condition."

"What condition are you talking about, Maggie?"

"Well, lass the condition of expecting a wee bairn."

"Maggie, I am not pregnant, I am just overtired and worried about my husbands."

"Lass, I have never been wrong yet, wait a few weeks and you will see."

Crazy lady, I cannot be pregnant. I only had a monthly couple of weeks ago.

I shake my head and watch Maggie make breakfast. Maggie is a whirlwind in the kitchen, she flits about around her husband cleaning up behind her, so as not to intrude on her husband working.

She is like a hummingbird, I wish I had her energy.

She hands me a plate of fluffy pancakes that make my mouth water with every bite, they are smothered in honey and topped with finely chopped fruit.

"These are delicious, you must teach me to make them."

"Family secret recipe my dear, I will tell you one day, now stop wallowing in worry and go to the library and pick out a good book, it is the door next to your room, the fire is going so it should be warm enough in there, but there are blankets on the chair and I will bring you some tea shortly."

I walk away despondent, feeling lost as I leave the room, I hear Maggie whisper.

"Poor young lass, her husbands of hers have got her all in a twist, I hope they sort that job out soon or she will die from a broken heart."

Saddened at the statement, I go to the library to find myself a book and snuggle under the blankets and begin to read.

I must have fallen asleep at some point because the thud of the book dropping jolts me awake. I look around at the darkened room, I look at my watch and it is early evening. I stretch like a cat and rise from my seat. Maggie enters the room slowly with a bowl on a lap tray.

"Annie, you're awake? Would you like your dinner?"

"Yes I would, that would be amazing, is there any news on my husbands?"

She shakes her head sadly.

"I am afraid not, Martin has tried calling their phones and had no success, I am sorry dear, get some food inside you and you will feel a little better."

The soup warms my insides as I eat it slowly, savouring every flavoursome mouthful. Maggie sits with me while I eat, talking about the guys' childhood around the castle and how they used to terrorise the staff with practical jokes. The stories make me laugh so hard I have tears in my eyes. Suddenly Martin comes rushing in, he looks very pale.

"Martin, what's wrong?"

"Ma'am, I have not heard from your husbands, but a contact of mine has heard on the grapevine that there are fifteen men known from the mafia been sighted in London causing turf wars, with the locals, but the concern is they are known associates of Giovanni's."

I feel all the blood run from my face.

"Fuck, what do we do?"

"You stay here, while I travel to London and do some scoping, you are safe here as there are twenty-four-hour guards all around the estate."

I nod but my head doesn't feel connected to my body. Maggie grasps my hand, bringing me back to reality.

"Annie dear, you look unwell so have a laydown."

Martin helps me stand as Maggie takes the lap tray and I walk to my room, dissociating from the world and lay on the bed fully clothed, staring at the wall. I am covered by a woollen blanket, I hear the door click shut and I lay there wondering what has happened to Max and Ryan.

At two in the morning, I am pulling some skin-tight black, leather effect leggings on as quietly as I can, I put on a black cotton vest top and some flat biker boots, I grab a small rucksack and put my knife holster onto my thigh. My hair is as scraped back as I can get it and shoved into a ponytail. I creep downstairs using my phone as a torch, every creak and groan of the building makes me wince, I grab a bottle of water and chuck it into my bag as well as some cereal bars. I make my way to the front door, suddenly I hear someone clear their throat.

"Annie dear, where are you going?"

"I cannot sit here and wonder what is going on, I am going to find my husbands."

"I understand dear, now let me drive you to town to give you a head start, and please be careful."

"Thank you, Maggie, I knew you would understand."

"I understand but I still think you should let Martin do his job."

"I was kidnapped twice while Martin and his men were organising security, I would much rather handle things my own way this time."

"That is fair enough lass, but please come home safe."

"We all will Maggie."

We end up having to push an old beaten up land rover halfway down the drive before we start it up, to avoid waking too many people up. Its hard work, by the time we are driving down the road, I am sweating buckets. The journey takes three hours to the nearest town with a station, Maggie gives me a wad of money and says, "For the train and to help you get the boys back."

I take the cash and head into the station. I find a ticket booth and purchase a ticket to London, Victoria station, I then board the train.

I hope to God I can find them.

Chapter Twenty-Five

As the train pulls into London, I am fidgeting in my seat, I step onto the chewing gum and graffiti-laden platform, I pull out my mobile and look for a clue to where I have to start looking for my men, I end up deciding to travel to Ryan's headquarters for the building company and start there. Similar to the office I worked in, in the southeast, this building is mostly glass, stepping inside, I am greeted by a tall leggy stunning blonde who briefly makes me feel severely inadequate.

"Good morning, Madam, how may I help you?"

"Hello, I am Mr Matthews's wife, I need to go into his office to collect some bits for him, could you lead the way?"

"I'm sorry, Madam, do you have any identification?"

I hand over my driver's license to her.

"I am dreadfully sorry but this says Miss Delaney, not Mrs Matthews."

"Dammit, I haven't managed to change it yet, we only got married a few weeks ago."

"I am sure, Madam."

The woman's tone is beginning to sound patronising.

"WHAT THE EVER-LOVING FUCK, ARE YOU DOING HERE?"

I hear a shout behind me and I turn to see a very red-faced, pissed off looking Martin with about twenty men with him.

"Well, Mrs Romano-Matthews? What have you got to say for yourself? You are meant to be safe in Scotland."

"I am not some trophy wife who gets bossed around, I want my husbands back and I am going to help or so help me God they can argue with me when it's over. Now, can you tell this fucking praying mantis I am allowed into Ryan's office?"

The snobby lady tuts and huffs at my insult, making me smile to myself.

"Yes, Mrs Romano-Matthews is allowed into Mr Matthews's office even if he is going to kill me when we find him."

The blonde leads the way and opens the door, I step through only to see it has been ransacked.

"Martin? Come here."

"Fucking hell, I'm guessing someone has been here already."

"Why don't you ask Mrs Jobsworth who has been in."

Martin stalks off to question the attractive bitch. I look onto Ryan's desk and find a plan for a building near, where we live currently with a massive red cross through it.

That couldn't be where they were taken, it's too obvious, and maybe that's why the kidnappers want someone to know?

I grab the papers and run out of the office and steal Martin's keys for his car, and bolt out of the office and unlock the car, and speed off to the location of the plan.

Please be okay, please be okay.

My anxiety spikes as I get closer and closer. I skid onto the lane towards the build my heart racing, I pull up a little way from it and kill the engine, I tighten the holster and sneak towards the house, looking all around, I see about ten men walking around outside.

"Mrs Romano-Matthews, you are going to make me lose my job."

A harsh whisper sounds in my ears, and a hand covers my mouth. Martin followed me, of course, he did.

"I wanted to find Max and Ryan as quickly as possible," I mumble around his hand. I see movement all around us as Martin's men get into position.

"You are to stay behind me so you don't get caught in the crossfire."

"Martin, I will be fine, I have my knife," Unsheathing it as I explain.

"These people have guns, have you not heard the saying bringing a knife to a gunfight?"

"Martin, without my men I am dead anyway, so you do your job, I will do mine."

He huffs at me but draws his weapon, he signals to his men and we slowly creep forward. When we are a few metres away, Martin motions for us to go, I jump out, slitting the nearest man's throat as Martin shoots several men. We charge into the building and find a familiar woman clapping slowly.

"Tina? What are you doing here?"

I look at the woman, confused.

"My dear Annette, haven't you worked it out yet? You are meant to be the clever one."

Her eyes have a crazy sheen over them, she paces back and forth cackling like a witch, it makes the hairs on the back of my neck stand up.

"Annette, you stupid woman, you think you can commit murder and live to tell the tale? How very mistaken you are. I cannot believe you have not realised it yet."

She continues to ramble on to herself.

This bitch has lost her marbles.

I look over to Martin, who shrugs his shoulders looking as bewildered as I am. I flip my knife in my hands to settle my nerves and Tina's eyes flash to the blade.

"That puny little butter knife will not stop me, you have no hope, you dirty whore, you ruined the truce we had."

"What the fucking hell are you on about?"

"You really have no idea, do you?"

"No, you stupid twat, I don't have a clue."

"Well, this will be entertaining then," she doubles over as she laughs maniacally.

"You are starting to piss me off now."

She glares at me her eyes are bloodshot and her lips turn up into a sneer. Martin steps closer to me, causing Tina to charge at him, I step in front of him and slash at her with my knife, leaving a long gash on her cheek.

"You dirty whore, you slag, you cunt!"

She screeches like a banshee, clutching her face. A few of her men burst into the room and drag her out of harm's way.

"I will get you for this, I will scar you so badly you will be unrecognisable, so your men leave you, so you are so ugly and you will die alone."

Her screams get quieter as she is pulled away. Martin pursues them and I follow close behind, the men start shooting at us and we duck behind the back.

"Shit! They are gone."

"What?"

I run out looking for her only to see a black car speeding away down the road.

"Martin, you are gonna want to come to see this," One of Martin's men shouts from somewhere within the house. We sprint towards the sound of the man's voice, I am shaking hard and wobble as I run, Martin grabs my arm and holds me upright, bursting into the room I see a sight that no one should see. My handsome men are laid on the floor in a pool of blood, their eyes closed and large gashes on their heads, the smell in the room is rancid, I sprint to them and feel their necks for a pulse.

"Martin, they both have a pulse but it is weak, get them help now, if they die, what I did to Giovanni will be child's play compared to what I will do to you."

"Yes, Ma'am."

The next few hours are a blur of speeding cars and hospitals, I sit in the waiting room alone staring at the shiny pale blue floor waiting and praying for my men to pull through.

"Mrs Romano-Matthews? I am the doctor treating your husbands, they have both been in surgery for internal injuries, Mr Matthews had three broken ribs of which, one pierced his lung so we have had to re-inflate that, Mr Romano had the worst injuries of the two and had had to be put into a medically induced coma to help the swelling of his brain settle down, but I do believe they will make a good recovery, you may visit them now if you wish."

"Thank you, doctor."

I do not go and visit my men, instead, I leave the hospital unable to bring myself to see my strong men so unwell, I storm down the street and get a taxi home, my blood boiling at the whore who put my men into those beds in the first place. Once home, I strip off to my underwear and change from my bloody clothes to work out clothes and stalk to the gym, knife in hand, I charge at the punch bag slicing and stabbing, I scream out all my frustration as I do so, my entire body is a tightly bound ball of rage. Eventually, the punch bag gives up and sand spills all over the floor.

It wasn't enough, I need to kill Tina.

I roll my shoulders and shadow box with my knife, cutting and attacking the air.

"Ma'am, Tina has been spotted in one of Giovanni's old clubs, we are headed there now, you coming?"

"Not making you lose your job now?"

"After what that cheap hooker did to your husbands, I'll be holding her while you tear her limb from limb, your men may be my bosses but they are also my friends, I hate her as much as you do."

I quickly change into more club appropriate attire and run down the stairs to Martin. I put my knife away in its holster on my thigh and follow Martin to the car and hop in.

"This club is a seedy hell hole on a good day, so keep your wits about you and try not to turn your back on anyone."

"Yes, sir. Anything else I need to know?"

"Do not let Tina escape again, Ryan and Max cannot be as protected as I would like in that hospital, they won't let me post a guard by the room so we have men outside the hospital."

"Okay, let's sort this tramp out."

We drive to the run down side of town, where graffiti is on every building and a lady of the night on every corner, as we approach the club, the area gets rougher. The neon sign is partly broken above the door and the bouncer on the door looks like a human version of a pitbull. Martin clambers out of the car and waits for me to follow on my stupid heels, he raises his gun and shoots the doorman in the head and we all run in, I kick my shoes off as I want to be more stable on my feet. Inside is like a dank cave with sticky floors and dirty whores. I spot Tina immediately and storm towards her, grabbing my knife as I do, she cackles and points her gun at me.

"You can't kill me, I am carrying to the heir to the throne."

"What the fuck are you on about?"

"I have Gio's baby growing in me."

The fucking fruit-loop does a little jig on the spot.

"You fucked that snake? More fool you then."

"It means you can't touch me, I am protected by the mafia law."

I punch her in the head, knocking her out cold.

"I don't know about mafia law but that didn't kill you, but shut you the fuck up."

"Well done Ma'am, she was pissing me off too."

I look around and the entire room of Tina's men are laying on the floor bloodied and hopefully dead.

I must have been focused on Tina, I did not hear that battle go down.

One of the Martin's many men throw Tina over his shoulder unceremoniously and carry her away.

"What happens now, Martin?"

"We will take her away to one of the holding cells to determine if she is pregnant, if she isn't she will be disposed of, if she is we will keep her till the child is delivered, then it will be shipped to family in Italy where it can be raised properly, and then Tina will be disposed of before she can poison the innocent mind of her child."

"Fair enough, when you dispose her, I want to get her back for my husbands' pain."

"Of course, I wouldn't dream of denying you that right."

I begin to feel nauseous then and run to the decaying crypt which is the bathroom of this hellhole and throw my guts up.

Well shit.

I wipe my mouth on some bog roll. As I walk out to the main clubroom Martin looks at me, concerned.

"You okay?"

"Yep, just a bit nauseous."

"You sure?"

"Yeah, let's head home and ring the hospital."

We have to stop three times on the way home for me to puke on the verge. When we finally get back, Martin sends me to bed with a glass of ice water and rings the hospital for me to get any updates on my men. I am laid in bed when he knocks on the door.

"Yes, come in."

He slowly opens the door.

"Annie? Sorry, Ma'am, Ryan is awake. Would you like to visit him?"

"Yes, please, let me have a quick shower to cool me off."

"Of course, you get ready and I'll get you a travel mug of ginger tea to help settle your stomach."

I stand in the cold shower, my head resting against the cool tiles, my sickness passes and I exit the shower, dry myself and get dressed into a loose dress.

"Fuck me, this tea tastes rank, it's like fire."

"Don't be such a drama queen, it will heal your stomach."

I sip the burning liquid the whole way to the hospital, the sickness passes slowly. I enter Ryan's hospital room, he looks so pale but he is sitting up.

"Hi Annette, are you okay?"

"Am I okay? I should be asking you that."

"I am okay, just a little sore, now are you okay?"

"Yeah I am okay, I have been so worried."

"I am so sorry, I didn't mean to make you worry, where is Max?"

"He is in a coma Ry, I am so scared."

"Shit! I told him not to answer back at those freaks."

I lower my head and begin to cry.

"No, do not cry for us, come here."

I sit on the bed carefully as not to jostle his injuries. He kisses my temple and leans his head onto my shoulder.

"We are stronger than those arseholes, we will be okay. Now, where is that Tina now?"

"Martin's men took her away, she is claiming to be pregnant with Giovanni's child."

"That is just what we need, a claim to the mafia throne, I hope Max wakes up soon to strengthen his rule to put the traitors in their place."

I nod and stand and toddle over to the bathroom, I sway and begin to feel dizzy and the floor starts to come closer very quickly, the last thing I hear before I faint is, "Annette!"

Chapter Twenty-Six

Beep-Beep

I hear monitors beeping as I open my eyes.

"Annette, how are you feeling? You fainted in my hospital room."

"Ry, my head is pounding, can I have water?"

"No, we have to wait for the doctor to see you."

I look over at him and he is sitting in a wheelchair beside me holding my hand tightly, I close my eyes again to stop the light affecting my throbbing head. The doctor pokes and prods me, checking my blood pressure and taking some blood to be tested, his cool fingers press lightly on my abdomen and he writes something on his clipboard and smiles at me.

"Mrs Romano-Matthews, when did you last eat or drink?"

"I think probably two days ago I ate, and I had some water this morning."

"I see, you are probably dehydrated and in need of some food, as for the sickness, however, I need to wait for the blood tests to come back."

"Annette, why haven't you eaten?"

"With everything going on, I have been a bit preoccupied."

I snap at my concerned husband. He looks hurt at my sudden outburst.

"Darling, I am sorry, we never thought we would be away from you so long, please drink and eat now and get your strength up, we all need to be well for when the shit storm kicks off."

I huff and take a swig from a water bottle handed to me by Martin, who was keeping quiet in the corner. The doctor leaves with a smile on his face.

"Now, Martin, would you like to tell me why my wife was with you when you raided that rat hole of a club?"

"Ryan, sir, have you ever tried to stop her from doing something? I was afraid if I didn't take her she would stab me in my sleep."

"Ryan, I am right here, you could ask me why I went."

"Martin was meant to keep you safe. You are meant to be more sensible than that anyway walking into a bar with a fucking knife when they are armed to the gunnels with fucking semi-automatic guns!"

"Sir, I did offer her a gun."

"You be quiet, I still am yet to determine if you have a job tomorrow."

"Ryan Matthews, I swear to all that is holy you fire him I will re-employ him in my name, he did as I asked as you and Max were incapacitated."

"Annette, I am worried, these people are not a pleasant bunch, and we cannot lose you."

"I know how unpleasant they are, I've been taken by them twice before and saw what they did to you and Max so yes, I know how distasteful they are, this was my choice, not yours or Max's so suck it up buttercup, I am a grown woman who can make my own decisions."

"Annette, you could have been hurt or worse."

"Ryan, I thought you and Max were dead when I went into that room so to be perfectly frank I did not care about my own safety, I was avenging you."

Ryan huffs and rolls his eyes, giving up the argument with me, knowing I will not back down.

Knock-Knock

A timid-looking nurse enters my room with my chart.

"Ma'am, I have been asked to get a urine sample from you, I will leave the pot beside you and grab it in a moment."

Then she flees like a scared deer.

"I better do as she asks."

I struggle to lift myself off the bed.

"Martin, carry her into the toilet and wait outside for her."

"Yes sir."

"Martin, do not touch me. I can walk myself, I am not an invalid, Ryan, you cannot ask another man to help me to the toilet unless it was Max."

"Can't you for once do as you are told? You are unsteady on your legs and I do not want to watch you fall again."

"Fine, but Martin has to wait outside with the door shut."

Ryan smiles and agrees. Martin gingerly lifts me and carries me bridal style to the bathroom and shuts the door, he lowers me to the floor and I shoot him out and fill the cup.

"Martin, I have finished."

He opens the door slowly.

"Annie, I think you should stop winding Ryan up, you are going to cause the poor man to have a heart attack."

"As he should stop causing all this stress." I chuckle playfully and begin to try and walk back to my bed with the cup in hand.

"I don't think so, I am carrying you and your pee, so I do not get fired today." Sounding like a petulant child, I huff loudly but allow him to carry me, he gently lays me down and goes to look for the nurse to give my wee.

"Ryan, stop glaring at me, I am not a china doll that is going to break if I walk."

"You didn't see your head bounce off the floor when you fainted, I thought you had really busted yourself."

"I am fine, apart from my headache."

He scowls again but doesn't reply. Reaching over me, he presses the nurse call button and looks at me, expecting me to argue.

"Mrs Romano-Matthews, how can I help?"

"My wife is complaining of a headache. Can you please get her some pain relief?"

"No, sir, I cannot until the doctor has come back with her blood and urine results."

"Ryan, I am fine, I am going to have a nap till the doctor comes back."

The nurse hides her chuckle with a cough and leaves the room.

"Annette, sleep if you must but I will get you some painkillers soon."

I close my eyes and drift off. My dreams are filled with dark rooms and the sounds of my men calling my name. I am surrounded by Tina's insane cackling, which sends a shiver down my spine.

"Annette, wake up!"

I am shaken awake by my usually stoic husband.

"Annette, I swear to God, wake up, please."

"Mr Matthews, her body needs to heal."

"Ryan, listen to the doctor, Max will whoop your arse if he finds out you scrambled her brains."

"She was screaming in her sleep. Something was scaring her."

"Ry? Are you there?"

I open my eyes slowly, wincing a little as the light hurts my eyes. He stops shaking me and kisses me hard. I tap his shoulder, reminding him I need to breathe.

"Annette, how are you feeling?"

"A little better. How long was I out for?"

"Two days, the doctor said your body gave into exhaustion, he wanted you to wake up before he tells us about the blood and urine results."

"Martin, can you get the doctor for me? Ryan, is Max awake yet?"

"He woke up this morning, but the doctor said it will be several days before he will be fully lucid, he keeps jabbering about how we shouldn't have left Scotland."

"I agree with him, Ryan, I will go see him after the doctors come in."

"If the doctor says you can, Annette."

I roll my eyes and growl, "Overbearing arse."

The doctor strolls in and says to Ryan, "Mr Matthews, it is time for your dressings to be changed by the nurse, maybe your man could wheel you back?"

"Yes doctor, come on, Martin let's leave them in peace."

I look up at the doctor, waiting for him to explain what is going on.

"Mrs Romano-Matthews, your bruises and scrapes are healing well, but your fainting was from extreme exhaustion and dehydration. Now for the matter of the blood and urine samples, I am delighted to say you are expecting a child."

Sodding Maggie and her sixth sense.

"Doctor, do you know how far along?"

"I will be sending you for a scan in the next few hours, I know you will ask, yes you can visit your second husband as long as you do not overdo it."

"Thank you, doctor, and thank you for looking after my husbands for me."

"You are most welcome, now I will send Mr Matthews back in when he has had his bandages changed, he has sat by your bed the whole time. You have chosen yourself some fine husbands."

Ryan is wheeled into Max's room a little while later, I persuaded a nurse to help me walk there. When both my men are there, I whisper.

"I have some news for you both, I hope you are happy."

167

"What Annette? Is everything okay?"

"Yes Ryan, it is."

"Well, spit it out."

"We are having a baby, I am pregnant."

Ryan's face falls.

Oh shit.

"Ryan? Are you not happy?"

"You were fucking pregnant while fighting Tina?"

"Yes, I guess so."

"What the hell were you thinking?"

"Hey, don't you dare, I didn't know, are you happy or not?"

"We are going to be parents? That is awesome, Annie."

Ryan and I look at Max and I run to him and hug him tightly.

"Max! You are okay, thank fuck for that."

"Annie, watch the old shoulder that is sore."

"Sorry, Max, I am just so happy that you are both okay, even if Ryan is being a stick in the mud."

"Isn't he always?"

We all laugh together, a nurse comes in and takes me for my scan, and I promise the guys I will get a picture. I am blubbering as I look at the grainy black and white photo, our baby is tiny, about four weeks the scan tech tells me, I count back and that means we either conceived a couple of days before the wedding or just after, it is too soon to hear a heartbeat, but the measurements are perfect. The lovely lady prints off several pictures and hands them to me, when I have wiped the stupidly cold jelly off my abdomen. I walk back to my men, not waiting for the nurse.

"Well, what do you think, guys?"

"This child is going to be so loved, Annie. Are you feeling okay? Ryan said you felt unwell."

"Ryan needs to stop being a snitch, but yes, I am feeling much better, thank you."

"I am not a snitch, but yes, I am overjoyed to be a daddy. Now, Annette, you need to go get some sleep and some food and drink."

"But I don't want to leave, Max."

"Annie, I will be fine, go look after yourself and our baby."

I sulk and walk back to my room, sitting on the bed enjoying the vanilla ice cream Martin snuck in the hospital for me, when Ryan sent him for clothes while I was having my scan.

After a ton of ice cream and some ice tea.

Decaf, of course, the shite stuff.

I manage to have a shower and not puke or feel dizzy, the doctor says Ryan and I can go home. I am a bit sceptical about leaving Max but the doctor assures me he will be allowed home in a matter of days, while handing me pregnancy vitamins and some leaflets on what I can or can't eat, drink or do.

Oh, joys.

Martin drives us home with Ryan wincing over every pothole. When we get home, I get him his pain meds and sit with him on the sofa caressing my still flattish belly.

Hey, I'm a curvy woman without being pregnant.

Ryan's soft snores sound next to me and I cover him in a blanket and wander in search of Martin.

"Martin, can I ask you something?"

"Of course, Madam."

"One, stop calling me Madam, two, when Max is home can you take us back to Scotland as I felt safer there, I do not like being here, I feel on edge, and now with being pregnant, I have to be as safe as possible."

"I understand, Annie, we will see if Max is able to travel, then make the decision."

"I really do not want to be around here anymore and I grew up just down the road."

Martin sighs sadly and nods his head. He hands me a bottle of water and some tablets.

"What are these for?"

"They are pregnancy vitamins and some painkillers for your head."

169

I take them and thank Martin and head off to bed, my legs shaky from the long day.

I lay in my bed wide-awake, my legs twitching with cramps, I get up and walk around my room to get rid of the cramps, swearing to myself as the pain slowly subsides.

"Rough night, my love?"

"Yeah it is, my legs are cramping, and I was walking it off, why are you not in bed?"

"I missed my wife in my bed."

"I cannot share a bed with you Ry, I do not want to hurt you."

"Please darling, I need you next to me, please."

"Fine, but if I hurt you I am leaving to go back to my room."

He smiles and takes my hand leading me to the master bedroom where he went to bed, he lays back into the bed, sheets crinkled from where he lay before, I slide in as elegantly as my body will allow, Ryan kisses my cheek and smiles as his hand rests on my belly, and he begins snoring within minutes, with my husband asleep, I manage to fall asleep seconds after, the sound of his breathing soothing me into a restful slumber. My dreams consist of little toddlers with dark curly hair running through the corridors of the castle in Scotland. I wake before my serene-looking husband, his medication makes him sleep like the dead, I go for a walk around the house and I begin to make some breakfast, Martin walks in following his nose to the cooking bacon and eggs.

"Morning, Annie, Ryan. Sleep okay?"

"Yeah, he is still snoring, any word on my other husband?"

"He has surprised all the medical staff and is well enough to come home, your news of the baby must have perked him up."

"I will come with you to collect him."

"I don't think so, we do not know how many followers Tina had, and this whole ordeal has brought up some very tender memories for Max so we all need to be careful, and now you are pregnant, Ryan is back being a top dog so no getting around me now."

"Max is my husband as well, and they are both my child's father, I want to be there for both of them."

"Annette, the poor man said no, and I agree with him, you are with child so relax, Max will be here in a few hours then you can dote on him as much as you would like. Martin is only listening to the orders I gave him."

"Ryan, I am not your pet you can order around, I am your wife."

With that I storm out of the kitchen and go to the garage, I spy Max's sporty little superbike with the keys in. Reading the side I see it is a neon green, Kawasaki ninja, I grab a nearby helmet and swing my leg over, I used to ride as a teenager, to escape my mother's alcohol-infused rage. The rumble when I start it up makes my body sing with adrenaline and I rev the engine a little, then take off out of the garage and down the road to the hospital to speak to my calmer husband.

"YOU DID WHAT?"

"I took your bike and rode it here because Ryan said I couldn't come with Martin when he picked you up."

"Annie, love, I agree with them, it is too dangerous for you to be out in the open at the moment, especially as you told Martin how worried you have been."

"I am worried about you and Ryan, not myself."

"We worry about you and our child, please do not be so reckless."

"I want to protect our child as well, but I can't do that from being stuck on the sofa."

Max's face scrunches into a frown.

"You have to let Ryan and I protect you for once, that's what we are here for."

"I cannot lose you two, I have to be up and ready, not lounging about like you lot want me to be or I will go stir crazy."

He stares at me looking a little amused.

"You really are a stubborn brat, aren't you?"

I nod and giggle.

"Always my big bear, now if Ryan rings you haven't seen me, I wanna make the rude arse sweat a bit, I am going to ride to the chemist and grab some antacids and then go home, I promise."

"Fine, but please be safe."

"Hey, I am wearing the mafia ring, I am safe."

"That only works for people who follow the rules, love, but okay, I love you, I will be home soon to keep an eye on your misbehaviour."

I kiss him softly and hug him tightly, I walk out of the hospital with a weight lifted off my shoulders. I turn the bike on and speed down the road, the world passing by in a blur. I pass the chemist, I promised I was stopping at and continue on to an old friends shop. Joe owns a metalwork shop and specialises in making knives and swords for movies that are lightweight but still, if sharpened, are lethal.

"Hey! Joe you in?"

"Now there is a voice I haven't heard in a while, you well girl?"

"I am very well Joe, you?"

"Girl, I am always well, now you must be here for a reason, what ya need?"

"I am, I need a pair of lightweight throwing knives, the design is your choice but they need to be strong and sharp."

"Righto, lightweight steel, with a leather-bound hilt okay for you?"

"Perfect thank you, Joe."

"Any idea on the time frame?"

"Just as soon as possible please, there are some rough people after my family and I need to be able to defend myself."

"I hope your skills have improved girly."

"Yes, they have you cheeky arse, been training hard."

He lights the forge and gets the heat at the correct temperature, the molten metal glows a gorgeous orange colour. He pours it into the moulds and leaves it to cool, I love watching Joe work, I have known Joe since he was an apprentice and I have always been mesmerised at the beautiful, amazing skills he has.

"Red or black leather? Or both?"

"Joe, both please, sorry to be a pain."

"You? Never."

He braids the thin leather into plaits and winds it around the hilts of the knives to make them easy to grip, he hands my new knives to me and I see a rainbow sheen on the blades which Joe is famous for.

"These are perfect, Joe, what do I owe you?"

"No, do not insult me, call them a wedding present."

"Thank you so much."

"Now girl stay safe for me, I do not want to be attending your funeral next doll."

"I will, bye Joe."

He waves me off and I carefully put the knives into the saddlebag on the bike and head off to my next stop. Outside Ryan's office back at home, I take a few calming breaths before entering.

"Good afternoon Mr Matthews, I would like to know where Tina is kept."

"Annette, where the bloody hell have you been? Martin went looking for you at the chemist and you weren't there."

"Mr Matthews, please tell me where she is kept."

"Annette, please don't do whatever you are planning."

"Now Mr Matthews, I need to know."

"No Annette, please my love."

"Ryan, I cannot live in this area with that woman still breathing."

"Annette, we are sorting that situation."

"I cannot let my child come into this world if they have a target on his back."

"I feel the same, but we have to do this the mafia law way or we will have targets on all of our backs."

"Fine, you have two weeks to sort this or I will."

"Annette, I will do my best."

I stalk away like an angry lioness and go to my room and lock myself in. I take my new blades out from my jacket and lay them on the bed.

Joe did a good job here, they are super sharp.

I hide them under my mattress for safekeeping. I untie my hair and brush it with a hundred strokes to calm my anger a little, when that doesn't work, I have a cold shower and shave my body of unwanted hair. Once I am dried and dressed in some comfy clothes, I decide to go for a walk in the garden.

The dusk makes the walk better as the scent of the roses seems stronger as does the lavender, I go and sit by the pond where my beloved cat is buried.

"Luna, you would not believe how hectic everything has been, I am going to be a mother, isn't that amazing? My body is growing a human being."

If anyone saw me now, they would think I am crazy, talking to the grave of a cat.

I put my head into my hands and let out a small sob.

"I am so scared, Luna, I can't lose this baby as well as you."

I listen to the soft breeze dancing through the leaves on the trees and it soothes my soul. I calm my breaths and watch the beautiful rippling on the vast stretch of water, admiring the lily pads bobbing on the murky surface.

I can't stay here any longer.

I stand and walk back to the house to prepare to run.

Chapter Twenty-Seven

The drive on my beaten up ford fiesta is not a comfortable one, the suspension is very old and clunky. I am driving up to Scotland to stay with Maggie, I rang her as I left town and she told me I was welcome. The first hour of my journey was spent crying the regret of hurting my husbands weighing heavily on my chest, as I got further and further away I knew I was doing the right thing, as soon as Tina realised I was the person that ripped her man apart, the target would be on my back and my men would be more at risk as they would want to protect me. At least, she shouldn't know about the castle so Maggie and I will be safe. It is dark when my tires hit the drive of my destination and I breathe a deep sigh of relief. Maggie is waiting for me at the end with a young man to help me unload.

"Annie, are you okay?"

"Yes, Maggie, I am well just exhausted from travel, has the hidden room been set up for me as requested?"

I found the room exploring the last time I was here.

"Yes sweet, remember it locks from the inside so if you need anything from me you will have to unlock it, I wish you would tell me why you have run."

"I know Maggie, just know it's not the guys' fault."

Maggie sighs despondently and follows me to my hideout with my bags and some food for me to eat, the room has running water which is connected by a different line than the rest of the house so I will have plenty to drink and to shower and use the loo fine. Maggie hugs me tightly before leaving, I lock the door with several locks and begin to unpack.

I enjoy the food Mr McGraw made for me some hours later when I have settled in and had a shower. He made me some sausage rolls and some other pastries as well as lots of packaged foods that will last me a while. I look around this room, which is different to the panic room back home because this is bigger than most flats in London, this is just underground. There is even a small gym with a punching bag, treadmill and a row machine. For the first time in weeks I feel completely safe and secure, I made Maggie swear not to tell the guys where I am, she agreed after lots of persuasions. The bedroom is huge, it has a king-size bed and a large wardrobe perfect for me for the next few weeks.

I miss my husbands, but it's not safe till Tina is a problem solved.

I stroke my belly absent-mindedly, looking at my three knives laid out on the table and I begin to plot.

Not now.

I run to the toilet and barely make it before the contents of my stomach are lining the bowl.

When will this sickness end?

When I have finished, I wash my face with cool water and brush my teeth to rid myself of the wretched taste from my mouth, I sit down on the cool tiled floor and try to regain my equilibrium. The dizziness passes and I crawl to my bed and collapse onto it and go to sleep, exhausted from all the recent events, I wake once to the sound of my own screaming, the dream long forgotten. The next few days are confusing from the lack of windows in this place. I keep my phone on aeroplane mode so I can't have the guys contacting me, it tears me apart. Maggie comes twice a day with food for me and any essentials I need.

A week later, Maggie is due to arrive so I unlock the door ready and go and grab a glass of water, when I turn to head back to let my friend in, both of my husbands standing there with their arms crossed, looking like the cat who got the cream.

"Annie, did you really think you could run from us?"

"Max, Ryan, how did you find me? Was it Maggie?"

"Annette, we knew you felt safe here so would be a good bet you would run here, we wanted to give you space and wait for Max to be well enough to travel before we followed, and Maggie risked her job to keep your whereabouts hidden."

I stare at my feet, ashamed of myself.

"I didn't mean to hurt you both."

"Bullshit Annie, you didn't think we could protect you."

"No, Max I didn't, I also thought if Tina finds out what I did to her man there would be a target on my back which would risk you both."

At that moment, they both grab me and pull me into a bear hug.

"We don't care about the risk to us Annette, we want to be with you and our baby."

We stand for ages just holding each other till I pull away with tears streaming down my face, Ryan wipes them away before kissing me deeply and lifts me off my feet, carrying me to the bedroom with Max close behind. Ryan drops me onto the bed and lifts off his shirt, his ribs are still bruised but that does not distract me from the look in his eyes. Max groans as I wiggle myself out of my clothes. They both strip down to their boxers, both men are obviously hard, the thin material does nothing to hide their arousal. I lick my lips to wet my dry mouth and I tie my hair back with a tie from my wrist. Ryan grabs my head and crashes his lips to mine in a punishing but passionate kiss.

"Now, my little runaway, what shall we do with you?"

Max whispers from beside the bed. Ryan pulls back, my lips swollen from his kiss. Both men get onto the bed, Ryan moves to my head and Max to between my legs. Ryan flicks my nipples, making my body jolt and Max lifts me and grinds his covered cock on my already wet mound, teasing me. Max turns me so I am facing his friend and my back is flush against his front, he bites and sucks my bare shoulder, making my skin break out in goosebumps, his rough hands holding me tight so I can't squirm. Ryan then removes his boxers and starts to suckle my breast, his warm tongue circles my hard nipple. I feel Max shift behind me and when he stills I can feel he is naked also, his cock brushes at my pussy making my juices flow onto it.

"Ry, Max, please fuck me."

"No, Annette, you punished us, now it is our turn."

Max grunts in agreement with Ryan's statement. Ry pushes his index and middle finger into my mouth.

"Suck them."

My mouth waters as I suck, coating them with my saliva, Max teases my pussy by thrusting back and forward at the entrance of my pussy. Both men are panting now, struggling to maintain their composure. Ryan pulls his fingers out of my mouth and trails them down my neck then my abdomen and he stops just above my clit leaving my body denied again, I scream in frustration and both men chuckle. Max pushes the first inch into my body, making it open to him but not deep enough for any real fun. Ryan's fingertips gently touch my clit and he slowly circles around it making me crave more of everything.

"Please, more please," I beg loudly.

"Okay, you heard the lady Ry."

Max thrusts his whole member inside hard, he stays buried inside me not moving and Ryan rubs my clit a bit harder until I feel a familiar tensing and he stops.

"No!" I scream as the frustration gets the better of me.

"Annie, next time talk to us instead of disappearing."

He begins to thrust again, as Ryan speeds up with his fingers, both men working in sync, both with punishing speed. Soon I feel the fluttering again as my orgasm builds, Max pulls totally out of my body and Ryan stops his fingers.

"Please guys, I am sorry I worried you."

They snicker and move off the bed. I turn to look at them.

"Where are you going, guys?"

The men both have matching grins at my displeasure. Ryan reaches down to his trouser pocket and pulls out a blindfold.

"What's that for?"

Still no answer. Ryan covers my eyes and pushes me back to a laying position on the bed. I hear some metal clinking and then feel cool metal surround both ankles, my legs are pulled as far apart as they will go, I try to close them but find that I can't. A ball gag is placed into my mouth and fastened behind my head. Two sets of hands lift me and roll me onto my front, my knees are pushed forward so my chest is on the bed but my arse is in the air.

"Max, doesn't she look like a feast for the eyes?"

"Ryan, she looks good enough to eat."

I wiggle my hips gently, trying to stop the cool air from touching my aroused pussy.

Slap-Slap

A large hand swats my arse, making the skin sting.

"Keep still, my little warrior."

178

A few more slaps connect with my arse and the skin starts to burn with the rough handling, it is not overly painful but enough for me to suck in deep breaths. I end up unconsciously counting the twenty slaps that they give me. I feel a finger slide up and down my slit coating my lips in my arousal before pushing into my body. Another is pushed into my ass, my body is singing with arousal, my moans are hidden by the gag. Both fingers are removed and replaced with a cock in each hole, making me scream around the gag. They pick up the pace and my body cannot hold back its orgasm.

"Cum for us, show us what we do to your body, cum."

My body falls apart and I clench down onto my husbands cocks, they both grunt as my tensing milks them of their own orgasm. When they pull out, I feel their delicious cum drip out of me.

"Oh, dear Annie, you are wasting our cum."

I feel their cum pushed back into my holes and wiped around them, making my body clench in pleasure again. I am untied, the blindfold and gag are taken off me. I stay laid on my front and Ryan grabs some scented oil and rubs my sore legs. We all curl up together under the duvet, with me in the middle of my two men and fall into a post-coital sleep.

The following morning is like my runaway never happened, we all stroll around the gardens and enjoy breakfast outside, the men show me all the little hiding spaces for a good quickie, but when I ask what is happening with Tina, I am brushed aside and given non-answers. After the third or fourth time of asking, I get pissed off with it and shout, "For fuck's sake! Answer my fucking question, will you?"

"Annie, she is locked away don't stress yourself it isn't good for you or the baby."

"Max, is she pregnant? Is that why she is still locked up?"

"We don't know, she won't let us check."

"Do a pregnancy test on her."

"We have tried. She holds her pee in till we let her shower and then she pees in the shower, or pees herself a bit so we have to change her and wash her then she pisses herself fully as we get the new clothes."

"I say let her stay in her wet clothes."

"Sadly Mafia law stops us from mistreating her."

"What happened to these laws when Giovanni had me, or even the padre?"

"You were not our wife, so they had every right to do as they wished." Max kindly reminds me.

"I didn't see a wedding band on Tina's finger."

"When we raided her flat when we caught her we found a marriage certificate as well as the rings and some photos."

"Well, shit."

"Exactly my words, Annie."

"Max, we agreed not to discuss this anymore, Annette, you are carrying our precious child, we do not want to stress you."

"I will be stressed till Tina is six feet under."

They nod in agreement.

"Until we know one way or another, we cannot get rid of her or there will be a coup against Max and his rule."

I huff but don't say any more. I get a sudden sharp pain in my stomach and double over.

"Fuck that hurts."

Max grabs me and lifts me bridal style, Ryan runs ahead back indoors shouting for Maggie. I begin to scream, writhing and squirming in Max's arms, the pain unbearable.

"Annie, you stay with me alright? Everything will be okay."

I vaguely hear Maggie telling my men to lay me on our bed while she calls a doctor. My body tenses as the pain is overwhelming, I scream like a banshee and it echoes down the stone corridors.

"Maggie, will she be okay?"

"Let's wait for the doctor, dear."

Max lays me down as gently as he can and I curl up into a ball as tightly as I can. The doctor arrives soon after and checks me over, he pulls out a handheld ultrasound device and places it over my stomach, I feel a warm pool seep into my trousers.

"Mrs Romano-Matthews, I am afraid to tell you, you were pregnant with fraternal twins."

"Were? What do you mean were? That didn't come up on the scans."

"I am afraid Madam, you are losing one of your babies and one may have been hiding behind the other that is why it didn't show on your other scan."

I scream loudly, my world falling apart around me, Max climbs into the bed behind me and pulls me onto his lap, I kick, scream and bite to get away from him, my sobs wracking my body.

Max holds me tightly, not seeming to mind the abuse I am giving him. Suddenly I still and just feel numb and stare into space, my body making me go into a state of dissociation. I am somewhat aware of the doctor giving Ryan instructions on what to do now.

"In a few days, the bleeding will stop and she will be able to continue with the second baby's pregnancy to hopefully term, but she is not allowed to get stressed and she has to be on bed rest for the remainder of her pregnancy."

"Yes doctor, thank you, I hope that she doesn't fight us on the bed rest, as she likes to do."

"She can sit in the garden but one of you men have to take her there and she can take herself to the toilet or the shower, but she mustn't overdo it."

I stare at the doctor, my mind still in overdrive, he has short ginger hair that is in tight ringlets, he has emerald coloured eyes that sparkle with sympathy at the moment, and he looks in his late thirties. He leaves as quickly as he came. In Max's arms, my numbness snaps and I cry myself to sleep, my body eventually giving out to exhaustion. My dreams are bloody and gory, as I slit Tina's throat as she slits my own as I die in a pool of my own blood, I see two dark-haired boys, one with olive skin and one pale-skinned, watching me and Tina slowly suffocate in our own demise. The dream makes me jolt awake, wondering who the little boys were in the dream, I look down at my sleeping men and snuggle back down and fall asleep again, their soft breaths helping me relax.

Chapter Twenty-Eight

Eight months later

My pregnancy goes by in the blink of an eye, I am now eight and a half months pregnant and I look like a beached whale. Tina was pregnant in the end and she is due at the same time I am, so she must have conceived a few days before I put her husband on the ground.

I waddle to the toilet, Max chuckles. "Penguin." Under his breath, of course. I flip him off over my shoulder and go to relieve myself for what feels like the trillionth time that day. We found out a few weeks ago that we are having a boy, just like the dream I had many months ago. My guys have been amazing, they even brought some of the library up to my room so I wouldn't be bored during my bed rest. We had decorators in, making the nursery at the castle for our son, which I got to oversee, it is baby blue and grey, the walls are decorated with photos of the horses and some wedding photos. The Moses basket I brought online, of course, is a pale grey wicker one with white bedding. We are all ready for our bundle of joy to arrive.

Max guides me downstairs to the kitchen, the last few weeks have been particularly hard for me as I have ballooned in size, and I have been very emotional about said fact.

"Max, how can you and Ryan still love me at this size?"

"Annie, we find you fucking sexy carrying our child, you look downright ravishing with your pregnant belly."

Max's sweet statement causes me to burst into tears.

"Max, you made her cry again? Really?"

"I didn't mean to. She asked how we love her when she is pregnant."

"Oh, for God's sake, Max! You always make her emotional, come here, Annette."

Ryan takes me into his arms and hugs me tightly, his lips brushing my temple softly.

"Ry, I am a beached whale."

"No, you aren't Annette, you are our strong, beautiful wife who is making our life worth living every day."

This, of course, makes me cry harder.

"Annette, love, I think you have wet yourself a little, you have made my leg wet."

I look at the floor and sure enough, a puddle is at my feet and down Ryan's jeans. My stomach tightens in a cramp-like sensation and I groan.

"Guys, I don't think that was a pee."

"What do you mean, Annie?"

"I think it's time."

"Time for what, Annie?"

Both men stare at me, puzzled.

"The fucking baby is coming, you slow pricks."

They both jump into action then and Max races upstairs for my hospital bag as Ryan screams for Martin to bring the car around. My belly tightens again, causing me to pant and groan.

"Breathe through the pain, darling," Ryan says, stroking my back softly. The pain subsides briefly and we continue outside to the car. As I am getting into the car another contraction hits me.

"Breathe slowly, Annette."

"Ryan, if you talk about my breathing one more time, I will pop your bollocks."

"Okay, fair enough." He jumps away a little at my statement.

Max jumps into the passenger seat and we speed off towards the hospital, speed limits be damned. I have several more contractions in the car, when we arrive, Max grabs me a wheelchair from indoors and both men help me into it and Max wheels a screaming me into the maternity ward.

Bouncing on my birthing ball is doing nothing for my pain so the nurse gives me some gas to inhale, I take a deep breath in and nearly fall off the ball.

"This is good stuff."

I slur to my husbands, Ryan rubs my back as Max paces the room.

"Max, please stop pacing. You are making me dizzy."

He stops and sits beside me on the floor, rubbing my thigh.

"Fuck, fuck, fuck! Gas isn't taking the pain away now."

Ryan bolts out of the room to get the midwife, I groan and scream as my body tenses with the contraction. Max winces, hating seeing me in such pain, the midwife asks, "Mrs Romano-Matthews, would you like an epidural?"

"Fuck yes, please! Dose me up with all the pain relief."

She chuckles and helps me onto the bed before going to get the anaesthetist to insert the epidural. Both professionals enter the room and I am asked to sit up and hunch over, my men are standing in front of me looking rather pale.

"Sharp scratch, then you will feel better."

Fuck, that was more than a sharp scratch.

The midwife helps me lay back on to the bed.

"I am going to examine you now."

I nod, unable to speak at the moment and see her looking into my body.

"You are only six centimetres so try and get some kip."

I close my eyes and try and sleep, but I can feel two pairs of eyes watching me.

"Will you two fuck off to the hospital shop and get me a drink so you aren't watching me like bloody hawks?"

They both bolt out of the room, not wanting to piss me off. I try again to close my eyes, only to have a nurse come in and take my blood pressure. I give up trying to sleep so I read on my phone to distract myself. Ryan and Max gingerly open the door.

"We are back, Annette, we have brought you some water and some fizz as it is your favourite."

I smile and take the diet cola gratefully and take a huge gulp. In comes a doctor and midwife.

"Mrs Romano-Matthews, I am going to see how things are moving along."

Ryan, the poor bugger, is standing in the wrong place as the doctor checks my cervix, and he looks like he is about to faint.

"Don't you dare faint in here! Go up by your wife's head if you can't handle it." The midwife chastises.

Ryan shuffles up to the head end of the bed and kisses my cheek softly.

"Right, you are fully dilated, now it is time to push."

"But I cannot feel anything, how can I push?"

"Grit your teeth and push like you would do emptying your bowels and your body will naturally do the rest."

I grit my teeth as told and push hard.

"Don't forget to breathe, Madam."

"How come she can mention breathing but I can't?"

"Because, Ryan, she doesn't keep on at me about breathing," I mutter between pushes.

I pant hard and push again my body beginning to feel sore from the strain.

"He is crowning, keep going."

Max peers over to see.

"Fucking, hell, Annie I can see him."

I push again and again until I hear my boy take his first scream.

"He is beautiful, Mrs Romano-Matthews, a fine set of lungs on him, too."

I smile, exhausted.

"Would one of the new daddies like to cut the cord?"

Both my husbands go positively green with nausea at the thought, so the doctor cuts it and our son is handed to me and I start crying.

"He's finally here."

Our bouncing baby boy is taken away to be cleaned up when I have had a bit of a cuddle and a coo, he also goes for his newborn check.

"Guys, we have to name him," I say to my men.

"You name him, Annie. You have done all the work."

"I like the name Quinn Romano-Matthews."

"Then that is his name, Annette, it is lovely."

He is brought back to us and I hold him to my chest, he has Ryan's dark hair and my pouty lips. I try and feed him naturally but it doesn't work as he struggles to latch due to the size of my breasts, which currently look like Pamela Anderson's in *Baywatch*, so I end up bottle feeding him, which is better in my eyes as his daddies can feed him as well and have a closer bond with him. Max takes Quinn from me and snuggles him.

"Annie, you have done your part. Now sleep and Ryan and I will do ours so you can rest."

Before Max finishes his sentence, my eyes are closed. I sleep for twelve hours solidly, I wake to Ryan and Max shirtless.

"What the hell are you two doing?"

"The midwife said it was a good way to bond with Quinn, the skin to skin is soothing."

I smile at them for being so natural with our son.

"Guys, I need to pee."

Ryan hands Quinn to Max and goes in search of a nurse.

"Mrs Romano-Matthews, your husband says you need the loo, let me take your catheter out and then you may go."

She reaches down and slowly pulls the tube out of my body, she lifts the bag attached and says, "Good output. You can use the toilet regularly now."

Fuck me, it's like sandpaper that catheter being pulled out.

I swing my legs out of bed and try to stand, my legs are like jelly from the epidural, Ryan ends up scooping me up and carrying me to the loo, over his shoulder I see my bed is filled with blood.

"Ryan, stop! I will get blood on you."

"I don't care, you need help to the loo and anyway blood washes off."

I bury my head in his neck, embarrassed and ashamed of all the blood I can feel seeping out of me onto Ryan.

Ryan gently seats me on the toilet and stands outside to give me some privacy.

Ouch, that stings to pee.

I manage to wipe, wash my hands and go to the door.

"Annette, I would have helped you, while you are in there would you like a shower?"

"That would be amazing." I sigh gratefully.

Ryan strolls in, my blood on his arm and abdomen and turns the shower on for me, he sticks his head out and says to Max, "I am gonna help her shower when Quinn is asleep; can you get us some clothes and Annette a pad out for later."

I don't hear Max's response because I strip slowly and painfully, then I step under the warm water enjoying the feeling of being clean, Ryan washes me and himself slowly, letting me take my time. I look down and see lots of blood in the water and begin to cry.

"What's the matter, my love?"

"I am still bleeding, Ry. How is this normal?"

"The midwife told us while you were sleeping it can take up to six weeks to be fully healed."

"Oh, does that mean no sex?"

"Nope, no sex for six weeks, we want you to be fully healed, we cannot risk you getting injured."

I cry harder, a full snort cry. Ryan pulls me into an embrace under the steady stream of water and holds me till the sobs subside. I look up at him and kiss him deeply, which he returns for a while then pulls away.

"I love you so much, Annette. Thank you for giving us a son, you did well."

"I love you too, Ry. How are we going to cope without sex?"

He chuckles and kisses my head and reaches around and turns the shower off, first he wraps me in a towel and then himself.

"We will make do, anyway, Quinn will keep us busy."

We dress in the clothes Max must have left by the door and then go out to the room. Max and Quinn are both asleep in the armchair. I reach and gently lift my sleeping baby from my husband's chest and cuddle him gently, I smile at the precious bundle.

"Ryan, he is so adorable, I know I am biased."

"He is perfect like you, shall we put him into the crib? You need a couple of hours rest before we are discharged."

Ryan takes Quinn from me and lays him into the hospital crib as I climb into the now clean bed and snuggle down. I look at Ryan gazing at Quinn and smile sweetly.

My husbands are good daddies

Several hours later, Ryan has his arm linked in mine as we walk down the corridor to the exit of the hospital.

"Come on, Max, you won't break him."

Max is following us with Quinn in his car seat, he is holding it with two hands and walking very slowly, so as not to wake or hurt him.

"Will you two shut up? I don't want to wake him up, took me long enough to get him to sleep."

"Ry, I think the lack of sleep is getting to someone."

"Me, too."

Max glares at us briefly before continuing to walk like a snail behind us. When we finally get to the car, it takes both men to get the car seat into the car correctly, while I, on the other hand, sit in the passenger seat chuckling like mad.

"You two run a successful business and you get stumped with a car seat."

They manage it after a while and we head off towards the castle, we have made our permanent home for the time being. Maggie rushes out to greet us squealing about a wee bairn in the castle.

"Annie, he is beautiful," she says as Ryan carries the seat with Quinn inside, I waddle up the steps. Max holds my hand tightly so I don't fall.

Chapter Twenty-Nine

Ryan and Max take to fatherhood like ducks to water, they alternate the night feeds so I get a break. The first few weeks of Quinn's life go in a lovely blur.

When Quinn is a few weeks old, we decide to take him for a walk in his pushchair in the nearest town, so we load the car up with all the gear you need for a new-born and set off. The cobbled streets are not the easiest for me to push the buggy so Max takes over after five minutes to save my arms.

Ring-Ring

Ryan's phone trills, waking Quinn up so I take him out of the buggy and begin to feed him, I sit on a nearby bench to be more comfortable while Max stands next to the bench listening to Ryan's conversation.

"Martin, slow down, explain what's happened?"

"Shit, when?"

"Okay, we will be back soon."

Ryan hangs up the call and says, "We need to go home, something has happened."

We all rush back to the car while I am still feeding Quinn, we put all the stuff back into the car and I strap Quinn back into his seat when he is burped. Martin is waiting for us at the end of the drive when we get back. Ryan stops the car and Martin climbs in next to me.

"Tina has escaped with her new-born son, she had a guy on the inside who helped her."

"For fuck's sake, can't she just fuck off?"

"Language, Annette."

I can feel my rage start to simmer, and I shout, "Not now, Ryan, I am not in the mood."

"Annie, calm down. Quinn can sense your emotions."

We pull up and all get out, I hand the car seat to Max and storm inside. I change quickly and find the gym with the punch bag and throttle my frustrations out into it. Ryan comes up behind me and hugs my waist.

"My love, I know you are afraid, but please simmer down."

I continue to punch the bag with Ryan, trying to hold on for dear life.

"Will you let go?"

"No darling, calm down."

"No, Ryan, our child is at risk because of that fucking leech."

He lifts me up and pulls me away, I kick and scream, my eyes begin to water with pure anger.

"Annette, enough."

"No, Ryan, I told you to let me kill the bitch, but no, you have to fucking listen to the cunting mafia laws."

"Max's rule would have been compromised if you had, it would have made matters worse."

I let my body flop and growl with irritation. Ryan lets me go and I spin on him, my body shaking.

"Mark my words, I will kill the cunt before she lays a finger on my family, I will tear her limb from limb."

Ryan sighs in defeat and hugs me again. "We will be fine, my love."

With that, he leaves the gym and I continue to attack the bag until my legs can barely hold my body. Max comes and finds me sitting on the floor.

"Annie, do you feel better now?"

"No, I don't, how can we protect Quinn if we don't even know who to trust?"

He flops onto the floor next to me and kisses my temple.

"Annie, I am going to weed out the traitors myself, I have to go to Italy though. I do not want to leave you but needs must at the moment."

"Take Martin with you so you have some protection."

"I will take a small group of men with me so I will be safe, I have you Quinn and Ry to come home to, nothing is going to happen to me."

I nod and snuggle into him.

"I love you, Maxy, please come home safe."

"I love you too, now let's go find our son and have a good evening, I will catch the first flight out tomorrow."

Quinn is asleep when we find him and Ryan, Max makes us dinner and then we watch a movie on the sofa, I am sandwiched between my men and it kinda feels like the calm before the storm. I cannot concentrate on the chick-flick playing in front of me as my mind is going a mile a minute thinking about what Max is going to find in Italy when he gets there. After a while, I hear my men snoring and Quinn crying through the monitor so I go up to check on him, I carry his bottle up with me in case he is hungry. Standing beside my beautiful baby boy is none other than Tina, she is without her own son, which confuses me.

"What the hell are you doing?"

"My son is going to be the ruler of the mafia, I have to make this child disappear."

"I don't fucking think so," I say before charging at her and pushing her away from my child.

I pull out the knife I have always carried since the last encounter with this dirty whore and flip it in my hand. She notices the knife and pulls out her own, which is stained in old, crusty blood.

"No gun today, Tina? I taunt.

"Not today, I want to watch the life drain out of your eyes as you desperately try to save your usurper son."

I laugh darkly. "Not today, Tina."

I hope my body can take this, I overdid it in the gym earlier, I have to, I must.

She charges at me and I push her aside and she crashes into a chest of draws, she gets up wincing a little, a bruise already forming on her forearm. She charges again, this time managing to nick my side and I suck in a breath sharply.

"That is the first of many cuts."

Her eyes look crazy as she chuckles to herself, with her concentration lapsed I slice at her and leave a deep gouge in her bicep so deep you can see the muscle poking through.

"Ouch, you bitch! That hurts!"

She staggers backwards and leans against the broken furniture.

"Enough, Tina, you are not having my baby."

"That's what you think, my own child is hidden away from the likes of you and yours."

She lets out a piercing whistle and three huge men climb through the window, I grab my son and run as fast as my legs will carry me screaming as I go.

"Max! Ryan! Martin!"

All three men come running, they see I am being pursued and leap into action, when Tina's men see my husbands and their friend armed with guns, they drag Tina away back out of the window and into the night.

"Do not let her escape," I scream like a banshee and the men chase after them. I collapse to the floor clutching my now bawling son and cry.

"Mummy's got you, Quinn."

I sit there and rock him back and forth till he settles again. When he has stopped crying, I take him downstairs and make him a bottle and I sit feeding him. Maggie comes into the room, crying hysterically.

"Are you and the bairn well? I heard all this commotion and came running but I was stopped by one of Martin's men saying Tina was trying to take Quinn and he wouldn't let me past."

"We are okay, my husbands and Martin are trailing them so hopefully they will get her once and for all."

"My dear, you are bleeding."

I hand Quinn to her and check my side, sure enough, blood is dripping down my side and seeping into my clothes. Maggie lays Quinn in his downstairs Moses basket next to me and grabs me some antiseptic wipes to clean myself up with.

"It's not too deep, Annie, you shouldn't scar."

"Tina will, I cut deep into her arm, I could see her muscle moving."

"As much as that mental image disgusts me, good on you for cutting her."

Maggie puts a dressing over my now clean side and pats my shoulder.

"I hope the guys catch her this time, Maggie, it is getting old now, this cat and mouse chase, and it was bad enough with Giovanni."

"Let's hope, Annie, Martin said she had a man on the inside, when she escaped."

"Yes, he let her out."

"I bet it was that bloody Timothy, he was a member of one of the old families that followed the padre, the terrible man he was, little Timmy became like a brother to Giovanni, they were inseparable."

"I will tell the guys when they get back."

Maggie smiles at me. "I am going to prepare the panic room for you and your sweet child to stay in tonight as we don't know where Tina is hiding."

"Thank you, Maggie, you really are the best."

"I know, dear."

I chuckle and follow her, carrying the Moses basket with Quinn inside. Maggie opens the door for us and rushes to and fro with food, blankets, clothes and all of the essentials I need for my baby. She hugs me tightly and whispers.

"They will be back soon, don't you fret, you care for your boy and we will all protect you."

"Please be safe, Maggie, I do not want to lose any of you," I say tears coming to my eyes.

"Now, no tears for us, go hold your baby and we will come for you soon."

I nod, closing the heavy door I check every lock twice before curling up on the sofa with Quinn using his presence to calm me. I look at his now dark curly hair that is growing like mad, his blue-green eyes look like my own. I kiss his head and sing softly to him before laying him back down. I check my phone for messages, finding it empty, my heart sinks and my panic rises as minutes turn into hours with no contact. I end up having to have a freezing cold shower to cut a panic attack off at its roots. I braid my hair as a grounding exercise and to keep me busy. I then get into bed and try to sleep, my brain is in overdrive, worry racing round and round. I stare up at the ceiling, trying to let exhaustion overtake me. Sometime later, I hear loud banging on the door. I go to open it.

"Who is it?"

"Annie! They are back, they are home."

I undo all the bolts and grab Quinn and race to my husbands, I skid to a stop just in front of them, they are covered in blood, what looks like their own and another's, I hand Quinn to Maggie and run to my men hugging them both tightly.

"You are home, you are here."

"We are home, Annie, be careful. You will get blood on you."

"I don't care, you are home."

"Annie, Tina got away, with only one of her men, but she got away."

"What happens now?"

"Annette, Tina has broken the very rules she was using to protect herself, so now she is fair game."

I grin widely and whisper. "Now it's my turn to protect you two."

I walk away in search of my blades. In my room, I change into tight-fitting, easy to move in clothes and strap my knives to my body. On the way out the door, I am stopped by Max and Ryan.

"Where do you think you are going?"

"Ryan, I am going to remove Tina from God's green earth, where did you think I was going?"

"Annie, I know you will fight us till you are blue in the face and then ignore us and do what you want anyway, so take some men with you, we will be here when you are ready to return."

I stare at Max gobsmacked that he isn't arguing with me.

"No, I am not letting her go, we are going with her, and Quinn will be safe with Mrs McGraw, for a few weeks until everything is safe," Ryan says scowling at Max for his suggestion.

I ponder for a few moments weighing up the pros and cons.

"Okay, Quinn stays here, I've had an idea, the padre, the delightful man he was, had dogs to track me when I escaped, any chance you have access to them, Max?"

"When the padre died, most of them were killed, I think there is a few left, and I will make a few calls and get them here to track this bloody woman down."

"Good, Maggie, you, Quinn and Mr McGraw lock yourself down in the panic room until we come back. Do not open that door to anyone but us three."

"Yes Ma'am, we will protect your boy with our life."

"Let's hope it doesn't come to that."

We all separate and I help Maggie stock the panic room with everything they are going to need, I even go to the nearest town and buy ten boxes of baby formula, some extra blankets and tinned food. I put it all away and hug Maggie and Quinn tightly, Max appears in the doorway.

"Annie, it's time to go, the dogs have got a scent."

I kiss my boy on his head and follow his father out of the room, I hear Maggie lock the door, which fills me with a sense of relief.

My son is safe, my son is safe.

I take a deep calming breath and pull my hair up into a bun so it is out of my face, we meet Martin at the front door there are about ten dogs with handlers, barking and snarling all looking in one direction, the way that Tina ran.

"Ready? It's going to be a long few days, it's mainly on foot, we have a few guys in cars if you get tired, Annie."

"I'm ready." My voice is monotone as I concentrate on the dogs that are now my lead to the woman I am going to wipe off the face of the earth. There is a

194

shout from the main dog leader and we are off, I keep a steady pace jogging behind the dogs, the sound of their barking is deafening. We enter a forest a mile away from the estates ground and the dogs begin to run as the scent is fresher here, I pick up my speed to keep up.

"Annie, are you ready for this it is going to be brutal, Tina brought more men over that had Giovanni's back, here take these."

Max hands me a set of brass knuckles, they are thinner than ones I have seen before, and they have a vine pattern on, so at once I know he had them made for me.

"Thank you, Max, love you."

Ryan stops me and kisses me deeply.

"I love you, Annette, we will get through this."

We continue on for several arduous days and suddenly the dogs all stop and go deathly silent. Martin approaches us quietly and whispers.

"We are about a hundred metres from what looks like an old military base that has recently been brought, as there is a for sale sign on the chain-link fence, looks like we found Tina."

I smile, excited to finally have all the bullshit over with, Martin cuts a large hole into the fence to let everyone through.

"On my signal, we will take the place by surprise, we hopefully will have better odds that way."

Ryan explains as I pull my twin blades from Joe, out of the strap on my waist I had concealed earlier. Ryan raises his fist and we all still, he drops it and we charge, Martin kicks down the door and everyone piles in, dogs and all. The first man I see, I stab in the neck and race past. I feel a hand grab me and I spin on him, a hulking man sneers at me, his fist flying towards my face, I duck and stab him in the gut causing him to double over, his hand on his wound, he tries to draw his gun and I stab him in the eye, as I withdraw my blade from his head his eyeball comes with and I have to shake it off my blade.

Yuck!

Ryan and Max are fighting beside me, I watch a man with blonde hair trying to sneak up on Max so I throw one of my knives causing it to stick into his back, I sprint over and slice his ear off with my other blade while removing the one from his back, he flops to his knees as Max finishes with the man he was fighting.

"Good job, Annie, keep going." My darling husband encourages.

I flex my hands, feeling the brass on my knuckles. A woman screeches at me running at me at full speed, I move to the side and watch as she trips over her own feet in a panic to get me down, I follow her down punching her face, enjoying the satisfying crunch as my knuckles connect with her cheek. I hit again, this time her nose, it breaks with one hard connection from my fist. When I am finally satisfied that she is out, I continue on stabbing and hitting my way through, a few people get a few hits on me, but nothing is going to slow me down to get my revenge. I burst through a door at the end of the long corridor to find Tina surrounded by ten large men with machetes looking rather intimidating. Ryan and Max follow me in, our men file in behind us, and the small room begins to feel rather claustrophobic.

"Well, well look what the cat dragged in boys, the whore and her husbands wanted to pay little old me a visit, thanks for the dodgy arm, but I will still take you no problem."

"Tina, let's settle this properly, you and me, there is no need to waste our men's lives." I try to sound strong but indifferent to this woman, I keep my head held high.

She stands bolt upright and her face lights up in a slow grin.

"Sounds perfect woman to woman, let's go to the old canteen. There is more space."

She leads the way and we all follow behind closely, the canteen is huge with a tall ceiling, I try not to show my exhaustion.

"Is this not a perfect arena for our final battle?"

"Let's just get on with it." Irritation seeps into my voice.

I shrug off my jacket and roll my shoulders ready to do battle. Tina produces a long hunter's type blade from somewhere on her person and swings it in a circular motion to show how she is trained with that blade. I space my legs apart to make myself more balanced and wait for Tina to attack. Of course, Tina's crazy addled mind makes her sloppy and she races towards me knife raised leaving her stomach and legs unguarded, I sidestep step letting her run past, like a matador and a bull. As her back is turned, I take a swipe with my twin blades, leaving twin wounds down her back, making her roar with a mixture of pain and anger. She turns, her posture slumped slightly and she charges again, this time the knife is lowered a little, so I slice down her cheek. I get a bit cocky and the next time she runs at me she manages to slice my thigh, I grit my teeth through the pain, not wanting to show weakness to the psychotic tramp. She notices the blood on my leg and chuckles.

"Not so invincible now, eh? Giovanni told me you were a fighter. Maybe when you're done, my patient men can have a turn and make your dear husbands watch, it will be amazing watching your resolve crumble to dust as your body is abused."

"Never!"

I pretend to drop one of my knives as she gets closer to me again, her smile widens, I catch it just below her waist height and stab it up into her gut causing her to choke, she embeds her knife into my shoulder, causing me to actually drop a knife, I swing my injured arm and hit her temple with my brass knuckles causing her to step back. I feel the warmth of my blood trickling down my back as I step forward and punch her again, this time connecting with her cheek. She spits at me her saliva filled with blood. I can feel my body shaking with overuse.

I have to finish this quickly or I am in trouble.

I lift my hand with my blade in and slice it across her neck. Her life's blood pours onto the floor, coating me in the process, I drop to my knees as her body collapses. Tina's men scatter apart from three very tall, very large looking Italian men, they stand stock still with their arms crossed, and their unemotional faces make the hairs stand up on my neck.

One of the men draws a pistol from behind his back, Ryan drags me out of the room, kicking and screaming, Max and Martin raise their guns, my heart is in my mouth at the suspense. Ryan manages to get me out of the room, I begin to panic that I cannot see what is happening.

"Calm down, Annette, we need to get you to safety."

"No, I can't leave Max, no."

I try to run back to the room. We get halfway out when I hear shouting coming from the room we just left.

"Ryan, we need to help them."

"Annette, they will be fine. They are both competent with a gun, Max will not leave you without a fight, my love."

"I cannot lose him, Ry, I cannot lose either of you, my heart can't take it."

Ryan hugs me tightly and kisses my forehead.

"You won't lose either of us, I promise."

Bang

"What the fuck was that? Ry, please tell me who it was."

Bang-bang-bang

I race back towards the canteen with Ryan trying desperately to stop me from entering the room, Martin rushes out to meet us, he is covered in blood.

"Max has been hit. I managed to kill two of the men, but his shooter got away."

"What about your fucking promise now, Ryan?"

I barge past Martin, who tries to grab me and stop me from seeing the room. I stop at the sight of my perfect, bear-like husband laid on the floor in a pool of his own blood, I rush up to him and try to find a pulse, I feel a faint thrumming in his neck.

"Martin, Ryan, he has a pulse but it is weak."

Both men rush beside me.

"Martin, get Max to a hospital, I need to get Annette there, he is losing too much blood from his shoulder, get him there safely, you will have her to deal with if he dies."

Martin nods and begins to drag my bear away, telling him he has to wake up to see his son grow. I stand and feel a little woozy from blood loss and turn to Ryan.

"I don't feel so good."

The last image I have before succumbing to the darkness is Max's lifeless body covered in blood being dragged away.

The End, for Now